"Go, go, go!" Brock screamed.

The pilot took the chopper airborne and as they raced up over the canopy of trees below, Anna caught a glimpse of the second helicopter coming up behind them.

Brock sat down beside Anna.

"I've had bad dates before, Quick," Brock yelled over the roar of ammunition firing, "but this is ridiculous."

"Sorry about that," she yelled back. "I'll try for dinner and a movie next time."

"I'm going to hold you to that."

"I hope you do."

Suddenly, there was an intense shudder in one of the engines, followed by violent shaking. It didn't stop. Brock's eyes widened.

Anna could hear the pilot shouting into the radio before he turned to them and hollered, "We're going down. Hang on. It's gonna be a rough—"

Dear Reader,

I'm surrounded by Bombshells so it was easy for me to write about one. Between my wife, daughter and daughter-in-law, I had plenty of material to draw upon to create Anna Quick. She's a combination of all three of these dynamic women, with a touch of mama-bear-defending-her-cubs just for fun.

I hope you enjoy reading about Anna and her adventure as much as I enjoyed writing about her.

Best,

Terry Watkins

THE
BIG
BURN

TERRY WATKINS

Published by Silhouette Books

America's Publisher of Contemporary Romance

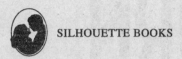 SILHOUETTE BOOKS

ISBN 0-373-51390-9

THE BIG BURN

Copyright © 2006 by Rick Watkins

www.SilhouetteBombshell.com

Printed in U.S.A.

TERRY WATKINS

as a high school student spent time tracking and camping in the mountains of Pennsylvania. Later he would do just about everything, from serving his country in the military to earning an MFA in writing from the American Film Institute. He's credentialed in industrial firefighting and has carried a top secret clearance for work as a security officer. Settled now in San Diego with his wife, author Mary Leo, Terry is busy putting his love of action-adventure into novels.

For Aaron: beloved son, friend and teacher.
1970–2005

Prologue

Kuala Lumpur, Malaysia

Jason Quick pulled the laptop from the bloody hand of the dead Malaysian, then rifled through the man's pockets until he found the keys. They were in the right-hand pocket of his jacket. The key ring held the JumpDrive memory stick Jason was hoping for. A backup for the laptop. He quickly yanked it off the ring and started down the alley where a car waited.

The nervous-looking Malaysian standing beside the car yelled at him in Malay, urging him to hurry. Another man, sitting behind the wheel, also insisted that he hurry.

Jason was about ten yards away from the car when

he heard shouts behind him. He turned just as a man came after him, firing his weapon.

Jason felt the searing pain of the bullet as it went through the inside of his left thigh.

He spun, dropped to one knee and fired three rounds.

His pursuer went down—only to be replaced at the mouth of the alley by two more men trying to stop him.

More gunfire erupted.

The Malaysian waiting for him at the car returned the gunfire, while Jason rose and limped toward him. Bullets screamed both ways, pieces of stucco flew from the walls, men yelled obscenities in Manglish, the Malay's version of English, and a perfect description of the mangled combination.

The passenger car door opened and Jason dived inside.

His Malaysian partner, now hunkered down on the ground beside the passenger door, was hit twice. As Jason tried to get him inside, the car lurched forward and the man slipped from his grip.

He had no choice but to leave him.

"Get the hell out of here! Go! Go! Move it!" Jason yelled while turning to look behind them as their car blasted out of the alley and then swerved through the clogged streets of Kuala Lumpur. He could see the great towers behind him, tallest buildings in the world. And he could see a black car, a Mercedes, battling traffic to catch up.

He had to get to the dock. The speedboat was waiting. There was no chance of making contact now, of delivering the laptop to the right people. He'd have to get to the island and wait there until someone could manage to extract him.

Every terrorist in Jemaah Islamiyah would be after him. And every pirate looking to cash in. And the vast, well-organized crime syndicates working the Strait of Malacca, with its seventeen thousand islands in the waters of this, the most important oil and goods shipping route on earth, would be looking for him.

He held the coveted laptop against his chest with the protectiveness of a man who thought he was holding the living heart of Western civilization.

"We need to find my daughter," Jason said as the driver swerved to avoid crashing into an oncoming car, then straightened out and raced down the street.

Part One
The Smoke Jumper

Chapter 1

Southern California

Anna Quick felt a rude jolt when turbulence from an eighty-mile-per-hour gust of superheated air slammed violently into the jump plane. Her breathing was shallow from the tight constraint of the chest strap on the jump harness as she stared out the open door, the plane orbiting drunkenly over the raging inferno below.

A voice behind her said, "They're somewhere in that gorge, but there's no way out. Fires are moving in on both ends. It's going to blow up."

"How many people?"

"Four. College students on a backpacking trip. Two girls, two guys."

Anna nodded. They would be scared out of their minds, desperately searching for a way out. Then they'd face the realization they weren't getting out. Four college kids unequipped, unprepared. They would die the most horrible of deaths, screaming, choking, burning...

In the distance, two massive smoke columns broke through the inversion layer and shot hundreds of feet into the air. Tongues of fire snapped across the ridges and raced into the heavy brush and trees on the southern edge of the canyon.

The jump plane bucked again, with increased violence. The plane lurched sideways as updrafts of the ferocious, high-octane Santa Ana winds knocked them around as if they were a toy boat on a raging sea.

Anna's face and nostrils and eyes were dry and tight. The roar of the wind blasting from the gorges grew thunderous as the gusts hurled smoke and flames across the horizon. She studied the orange tidal wave as it swept up the slope of the mountain to the south, ten miles from the mountain community of Big Bear. She noted the axiom that every twenty degrees in hill slope doubled the rate of speed the fire spread. The vicious whirlwinds and updrafts were being created by the fire itself.

Anna processed the variables that produced this disaster: fuel loading, clear-cutting, weather, topography. In a decade of firefighting she'd never seen anything to match this. Her boss said it was becoming another Yellowstone disaster.

"Not going to happen, Anna. Back away from the door. This is a no-go," Carter yelled over the roar. "You can't risk it. I won't let you. There's no way out of that canyon now."

There's *always* a way out, Anna thought. The fire would burn over this canyon very quickly and the worst of it would stay up on the ridges.

"I'm going in," Anna insisted as she tightened her leg straps.

"The hell you are."

Another huge fire swept down from the north, threatening to marry with the one below, forging a giant tsunami of flame. Smaller fires snaked aggressively along the ridges, and out as far as she could see more flare-ups triggered by flying embers burst across the hills.

Anna Quick's team had been jumping small outback fires for twelve days. She was exhausted from slogging equipment up and down hills, digging, cutting, torching backfires. Behind her on the jump plane's nylon seats sat her seven teammates, tired, dirty and in a stupor only firefighters know. All they wanted to do was go back to base camp and collapse.

Anna, a lifelong mountain climber and college soccer star, had formidable reserves that gave her, at the most competitive level, more endurance than any other male or female on the strike team, but this time even she'd overdrawn her account. She was functioning on nothing now but sheer willpower.

"Dammit, Anna," Carter persisted, leaning in close over the roar of the engine, both of them holding on to the door frame for support against the slipstream and turbulence. "It's a no-go."

She ignored him as she pulled on her helmet, snapped the chin strap, dropped the heavy wire-mesh mask over her face and pulled on her Nomex gloves.

Carter grabbed her shoulder. "Abort now! That's an order!"

She stepped closer to the door, dropping into a sitting position with her legs out. She was going in light. She'd dumped all but the necessities into her PG bag and snapped it under the reserve chute on her belly. She had extra lightweight fire shields jammed into the nylon webbing of her Kevlar fire suit.

In the distance a superscooper dumped "mud" on the southern wall of fire. A futile gesture. Above the scooper she spotted a hovering chopper. Probably getting news footage, though it didn't have the coloring of one of the news birds. It looked military.

Her eyes focused on the horizon, searching for markers. The backpackers, communicating by cell phone, were last reported to be in the narrow gorge below, hiding in a dry creek bed. The fire would overtake them in a half hour or less. The heat and smoke would kill them sooner.

"Anna!"

She broke free of Carter's grip, pulled her legs up, got her feet under her and launched herself before he could stop her. She rolled out into the dark, choking sky, hearing nothing now but her own jump count:

Jump-thousand.

…now feeling the adrenal rush of the tumble into space, feet up, body twisting as she plunged.

Look-thousand.

...seeing now the earth and sky somersaulting over one another, the plane slipping past like a quick hawk, then seeing the fire.

Reach-thousand.

She grabbed the green rip cord. Windblown embers exploded against her mask.

Pull-thousand.

Her hand ripped across her chest.

The quick drop, then the tug of the blossoming round of orange and white canopy was always a beautiful sight to a jumper. There were no tension knots at the corners, and the steering toggles were okay.

She pulled directly into the wind as tongues of fire leaped up at her. Her gut tightened, her nerves stretched taut. The full fury of the firestorm mocked her descent toward the dragon's fiery mouth. It was starved for fuel, waiting to be fed.

At three hundred feet, she set up the brakes with the toggles halfway down, easing to her right, then left, reefing down on the toggles, maneuvering, deeper into the brakes, then full brakes as she zeroed in on her landing zone, a flat piece of ground.

Then, without notice, a sneaky backwind shooting up the canyon grabbed her.

She was in trouble.

Two thousand feet above the wildly gyrating smoke jumper, in an unmarked, Sikorsky SH-60 B Seahawk naval antiship chopper, John Brock held on to the frame of the open door with one hand. With the other he held binoculars, tracking the jumper's descent through the smoke as he held on against the violent rocking and rolling.

He watched in dismay as the winds grabbed Anna Quick's chute and drove her horizontally at great speed toward the slope and a stand of trees.

Behind Brock, a marine lieutenant was yelling on his satellite phone at some assistant to the director of Emergency Services at the California Emergency Control Center.

Through his headset Brock heard his chopper pilot declare, "That's suicide."

Brock had traveled twelve thousand miles to recruit Anna Quick. Wasted miles. He watched her vanish into the smoke. She was supposed to be on her way back to her base camp. Instead she was jumping into an inferno.

"She have any chance at all?" he asked.

The pilot said, "That's up to Big Ernie."

"Who the hell's Big Ernie?"

"He's the smoke jumper's god of fire. You gotta play the cards he deals. And he's a jokester."

Brock wasn't amused.

The marine lieutenant finished his conversation and moved over in the doorway next to Brock. Brock pulled back his headgear so he could hear the lieutenant.

"Sir, the strike-team boss ordered an abort. She disobeyed a direct order and went ahead and jumped."

Brock nodded. That was consistent with the file they

had on her. He swore softly to himself and continued to try to see something on the ground.

He said to the pilot, "Can you get this thing down there?"

"I can get it down. Getting it back out is the problem. Those Santa Ana winds are running sixty miles an hour down there. With low visibility and high winds the chances won't be good."

"I need that damn woman alive."

"Sorry, sir," the pilot said. "What you need is a miracle. The best I can do is to keep circling until the winds die down."

Brock stared in frustration at the gathering firestorm. He knew the pilot was right, that they'd have virtually no chance of getting to her and then getting out again.

The marine lieutenant said, "That's got to be the worst way to die."

Angry as he was at the woman's defiant jump, Brock couldn't help but admire her courage. As an operator with Delta Force, Brock had gone into his share of extreme-risk situations and he knew the kind of mind-set that it took. She had to know something about the conditions, something no one else was taking into account. Either that or she was suicidal. He hoped for the former. He hadn't come all this way for a charred corpse.

All attempts by Anna to keep her direction, to lock in the topography, had been blown away, and now she was in the hands of the wind. A vicious gust spun her around and she had to fight the near collapse of her chute.

It was now a desperate battle to get it under control. She was using every bit of her upper-body strength to keep the chute oriented.

When Anna found a break in the smoke, she saw the fantastic spectacle of fire crowning the treetops at unbelievable speeds.

The superheated winds buffeted her. She was engulfed in smoke, and for the moment, completely lost sight of the ground.

When the smoke cleared enough for her to see, it was too late. She sailed into a hundred-foot-high tree snag, her feet smashing through the top branches. Anna stopped with a violent jerk. The pads and Kevlar were all that saved her from being impaled. She still wore deep scars on her body from one such landing and was happy to have the new, stronger protective gear.

Anna looked up. Her chute was caught precariously. She looked down. It was an eighty-foot drop. Just great. She pulled out her drop-rope and hooked it up, released herself from the harness and began to rappel, trying desperately to get down before the chute gave way and dropped her like a stone.

She was about twenty feet above ground when the chute broke free. She plunged. Instinctively Anna pulled her legs together and angled them to the side in the standard parachute landing fall.

She hit hard.

Dazed, she rolled over and pushed herself up. The great fear of such falls was to have a sprained ankle or something broken. Anna made a quick survey of her body parts.

Everything seemed intact—until she rose to her feet. Her left ankle was weak. She skipped on it a couple times and decided it wasn't a disaster as she headed down into the deepest gut of the ravine. She picked up her walkie-talkie to let Carter know she was down. "Do you still have communication with the hikers? Over."

"Roger that. They saw you. They should be just up the ravine a few hundred yards."

"Ten-four. I'm on my way."

"Anna, I can't believe you just did that! The fire's coming over the ridge. Moving fast. You can't outrun it."

"I know, but I couldn't leave them down here."

Anna reached into one of the inner pockets of her jumpsuit and took out a small pair of binoculars. She tracked along the ridgeline, acknowledging the treacherous beauty of the snaking line of fire, then she tracked down the hills into the gorge. How a fire feeds depended on where the fuel load was the heaviest, plus how the winds were directed by the lay of the mountains, and where inversion would multiply velocity.

What she was looking for was an area where the fuel load would be the least, the topography the easiest for the fire to quickly burn over.

When she turned and looked up the canyon, she saw the students running toward her. Stumbling, falling, getting up. Panic-stricken.

* * *

John Brock watched the rolling fires converge and explode down the gorge in a swirling avalanche of flame.

He had the marine pilot circle for nearly an hour before the wall of flame had moved on and the winds relaxed enough for them to hazard a landing. The firestorm had left behind smoldering brush, burning trees and blackened ground.

"Nobody's surviving that for long," the pilot said as they made their descent.

Brock held out no hope, but he had to confirm the deaths.

The pilot found a flat, burned-over area where he set the helicopter down, the rotors blasting up a cloud of blackened soot and dust.

Brock and the marine lieutenant exited the chopper, ducked under the orbiting blades and jogged away from the ash and dust.

He stared at the surroundings. It looked like a giant blowtorch had scorched everything. Embers still hissed and snapped like exploding firecrackers at the tail end of a Fourth of July celebration. Hundreds of smoke tendrils drifted skyward.

Brock tracked back and forth along the canyon and the arroyo as the acrid smoke wreaked havoc with his sinuses and eyes. "The bodies have to be around here somewhere," he said somberly, then sneezed.

They began the melancholy search. Brock was moving along a dry, shallow creek bed, when he stopped. Dirt under an overhang just ahead of him moved. It occurred to him that he might be looking at the covered den of a mountain lion.

When the dirt and ash moved again he started to ease his hand toward the 9 mm Glock in the shoulder holster under his left arm.

He stared drop-jawed at what he saw next. They came out one at a time, dirt and ash falling off their protective shields. All of them. All five.

The college students appeared to be in total shock. They stared silently, amazed to be alive.

The one in the fire gear barked orders like a drill sergeant at her rescued lambs, telling them to pack the heat shields and whatever else was on the ground that wasn't burnt up. She had to be Anna Quick.

She was a tall, striking woman, even when covered in ash. She wore her golden-brown hair short and had a confident swagger as she walked toward him. She was prettier than the picture they had on file.

"You are, I believe, Anna Quick?" Brock asked.

"I am. And I appreciate whoever you are for getting here so fast."

She turned and started to direct the college kids to the chopper.

"We're not the rescue team," Brock interrupted, then radioed the chopper pilot who told him a rescue bird was on its way. Brock then relayed that information to Anna.

They ducked away from gust of ash the wind had kicked up.

"If you aren't here to help, who are you? And what are you doing here in the middle of this mess?"

"My name is John Brock. I came here especially for you." He showed her a Military Intelligence ID.

She studied it for a moment, then handed it back. "What could Military Intelligence possibly want with me that's so important they'd come looking for me in the middle of a fire?"

"We need your help. Or, more specifically, your father needs your help."

So much for the *intelligence* part. These guys were wrong. "My father's presumed dead. Has been for the past eight years or hasn't anyone bothered to pass that information on to you?" It came out harsher than she'd meant it to, but she was exhausted. She turned to walk away.

"Well, actually he's not dead. At least not yet."

Chapter 2

Anna tried to absorb what this guy was telling her. There wasn't any chance that it was some kind of bad joke. He didn't look like the joke type. Plus, he had a chopper, a marine officer accompanying him and the official ID. No, he was on the level.

Her father was alive? Given what she'd just gone through with the fire, dealing with this news was almost more than she could get herself around. She needed a moment for it to settle in.

"Let me take care of my business here—" Anna gestured to the students "—before I deal with this, if you don't mind."

"Go ahead."

"Do you think you can spare some water?"

"No problem," Brock said, and asked the marine to see what was on their chopper.

For the next fifteen minutes Anna stood with her group while each of them tried to make cell-phone calls to desperately worried parents and friends. The conversations touched on how great their rescuer was.

Their attitudes, now that they were assured of certain survival, became jovial. They had a great story to tell and they were already getting into it.

Meanwhile, the marine lieutenant, square jawed and rather gaunt-looking, fetched some much-needed water bottles and passed them around. Anna quickly guzzled one and went for a second.

John Brock was off pacing and talking on his cell phone. Occasionally he'd glance over at her as he talked, nod, as if she was the topic of conversation. He was well over six feet, had a beach tan and had gone a day or two without a shave. He sported square sunglasses, a loose-hanging blue shirt and khaki pants with side pockets.

When the rescue chopper appeared and landed on the valley floor, the hikers headed for it like refugees from a dying planet. While the students boarded, Anna finally turned and walked over to Brock. He had that look of someone who'd seen and done things that you would never hear about in the light of day.

She took a deep breath and said, "Okay, you're telling me my father is alive, which I don't believe. Was he a prisoner somewhere? Is that why he's been missing all this time?"

"No. Not exactly. But that's a story for another time.

Right now he's in trouble and we need to get to him as soon as possible."

"Where is he?"

"Malaysia."

"My father's alive in Malaysia, and he's in trouble? You came all the way out here to tell me that? I don't understand."

"You will."

She brushed ash from her face and ran her tongue over her now extremely chapped lips as she struggled to get a grasp on what this man was telling her.

"When?"

"We're here to take you to Miramar Air Base. You'll be briefed there."

She didn't like the sound of this. "I usually get briefed when I'm going on a mission. But not from the military. I'm not in the military."

"Actually, it's a CIA mission. And I'm pretty sure you'll want to go sign on. In fact, I'm positive."

Anna stared at Brock. Eight years ago, her father had disappeared in Southeast Asia on a secret mission with the CIA. He was one of a long line of smoke jumpers who'd been recruited over the years. They were once called "cargo kickers" and worked for the CIA's Air America, dropping supplies to pro-American guerrilla forces. Smoke jumpers were used extensively in the secret war in Tibet in the early 60's and the practice never really stopped. Since her father's disappearance, Anna had become an outspoken opponent of the relationship between the CIA and civilian smoke jumpers recruited into its ranks for special missions.

For a long time Anna had hated the secrecy that kept the truth from her and her mother. Though her mother and father had been divorced for several years before he vanished, they'd remained friends. Her mother was as upset over the lack of information as Anna. Divorce was hard enough, but his disappearance almost more than Anna could take.

The CIA had continually refused to tell her what exactly had happened to her father. The only official information she'd ever been able to get was that he'd disappeared on a mission.

"I want to know what happened to my father," she said to Brock.

"I'm going to tell you...on the way."

"To Miramar?"

"No. Guam."

Her throat tightened. She drank more water, staring over the bottom of the upturned bottle at Brock. The man never flinched. A real poker face if ever there was one.

She was unbelievably calm. Must be the exhaustion, she thought. Anna finished the bottle. "Why Guam? You said he was in Malaysia?"

"Guam's the jumping-off point. We've got a camp there. What we call an isolation camp, or IC. You'll be trained there."

A sardonic smile broke across her face. This whole thing was beginning to reek, and she wasn't in the mood for it.

"Trained for what?"

"Again, I'll tell you about it on the way. We don't have much time."

Until she knew more, Anna refused to succumb to his time schedule.

"All this robotic dialogue isn't going to work on me. Just tell me now, or you can get into your unmarked chopper and fly back to wherever you came from."

"Your father's situation is grave. We need to get to him. He's requesting you to help us."

"Why would he do that when he has the military at his beck and call?"

"We don't know why, exactly."

"You mean you won't tell me why."

"If I knew the answer, I'd tell you. We don't know why he's asking for you. We can only assume it's because he's trapped on a burning island and probably thinks you're the world's greatest smoke jumper. Personally, I don't buy it. We have the best jumpers on earth working for us and he knows that."

Anna hadn't had decent sleep in weeks. She was tired and dirty. That she was standing in a foot of ash in a burned-out ravine listening to this guy tell her not only that her father was alive, but he was trapped on some burning island and requesting her to jump in and get him out sounded, quite frankly, preposterous.

But if this guy was lying, why make up a lie so outrageous?

Unfortunately, he had the hook in her now and she desperately wanted to know the truth.

"I'll go to Miramar with you, but that's as far as I go without a better explanation."

"All right."

They both turned to wave at the rescue chopper as it began its assent. Anna watched it slant off into the sky carrying four very grateful people back home and wished she was inside that chopper with them.

Anna followed Brock and the marine lieutenant to the unmarked chopper, its rotors swirling languidly. The pilot turned toward them, the dark sun shield of his face helmet giving him a *Star Wars* look.

The flight to Miramar was a quick twenty-minute hop and Anna dozed for most of it. They landed and got out next to a C-17 transport plane parked just across from a squadron of jet fighters.

"This way." Brock motioned toward the C-17 as he walked. She followed close behind.

"Isn't there an office we can go to?"

"Not enough time. You'll be briefed on the plane."

"What if I don't like the story?"

"You can leave anytime you want."

She stopped on the tarmac. "Why do I have the feeling if I get on board that plane, I won't be able to get back off?"

He turned to her and pushed his sunglasses up on his head. "You saved four lives today at the risk of your own. That was no accident. I've read your file. When I tell you what's going on, you won't even think about getting off that plane."

"What makes you so sure?"

"Because there aren't just four lives at stake here, more like *forty thousand* lives. Including your father."

What? She couldn't think straight. Between the intense fatigue setting in and all the water she'd drunk, her bladder felt as if it was going to explode.

"I just really need a bathroom right now."

"There's a state-of-the-art bathroom on the plane."

She hesitated, looking around for an alternative, but the nearest building must have been a quarter mile away. She made the decision to go for the plane.

There were several men on board the almost barren C-17, hovering around a few laptops. She realized that the seats were all backward. Brock told her that in the event of a crash passenger survivability would be greater.

"Has that been proven or is that some military theory?"

"That's just what they tell me."

She ignored him and the men and went straight to where Brock told her the bathroom was located. She found the privacy she was looking for, shut the door and struggled to get her fire suit down.

The *state-of-the-art* bathroom was a hard, cold stainless-steel ordinary toilet, much worse than she'd find on a commercial airliner. But she didn't care. When she was finished she leaned against the metal wall, just to rest for a second—and fell instantly asleep.

She was jolted awake by movement.

Anna jumped up, struggled to get her fire suit on, fell back, but caught herself by grabbing hold of the sink.

Then, with her suit still around her ankles, there was a knock on the door. "We're going to be airborne in a couple minutes. You okay in there?" Brock said.

"Yes, I'm fine. But this wasn't part of our deal. I don't want to go—"

"You need to get out here and get a seat belt on."

Shit!

She pulled her suit up, then caught a look at her face in the tiny aluminum mirror. Somebody's face anyway. It was more like a clown's face with all the dirt and ash on it. She quickly washed as the plane rocked her back and forth. She wished she could strip off her grimy clothes and jump into a shower. Then when she was all clean again, she'd towel off and climb between silky cool sheets and sleep for a week. But she knew that vision wouldn't be happening for a very long time thanks to John Brock.

Her father's face flashed in her mind. She couldn't quite believe that he was alive. It made her delirious, angry, excited and confused—all at once.

When she finally emerged, Brock told her to take one of the empty seats.

"I'm not going until you explain everything."

"You have no choice. Make yourself comfortable."

"No beds?" she said sarcastically.

"Sorry, no beds."

He went and sat with the other men in the back of the plane.

Anna was furious. How dare they kidnap her like this? As the plane taxied up the runway, she realized there were no windows. It was a weird sensation sitting facing the tail of the plane as it taxied, and she didn't like having no way to see out. It gave her a claustrophobic feeling. This was all too much.

But she was just too tired for panic. After two weeks of riding in planes to jump fires, she told herself this was just another ride. And just another opportunity to catch a few minutes of sleep. As soon as they'd landed, she'd make them take her home.

Yawning, she grabbed a small pillow from the seat next to her, stretched out and fell dead asleep even before the plane was airborne.

Chapter 3

Anna woke to the steady hum of the plane's engines, the occasional murmuring of voices, but didn't bother to open her eyes. They felt as if they were glued shut and she didn't have the will or strength to force them open before they were ready.

Instead, she replayed the fire jump: cutting herself free, finding the students, calming their fears, getting them to trust her, the desperate digging, the waiting to see if they would survive as the fire blew over them, sucking out their oxygen and laying down intense heat.

They had been lucky.

"Hey, sleepyhead."

Now she opened her eyes as Brock dropped into a seat across the aisle from her. He handed her an open box containing a sandwich, a package of Oreos, coffee, creamer and sugar packets.

"It's not much, but it's all we have."

She accepted the offering, and dug right in. The hot black coffee tasted especially good. "Thanks," she said in between bites of cookie. "But this in no way changes the fact that I'm being hijacked."

"You boarded voluntarily."

"I had to go to the bathroom."

"Blame it all on your father."

She bit into a peanut butter and jelly sandwich. It was the first time in forever she'd eaten white bread and it tasted great. The whole meal was just what she needed to get her blood sugar going again. Straight to the sugar high, no stops for nutrition, then slow it down with the peanut butter. Get herself back on cruise control.

She was glad he'd left the aisle between them. Maybe he couldn't smell her sweat-laden body odor the way she could.

"I'm going to tell you far more than I normally would, or should," he said. "That's because of the abnormal circumstances involved. Your *need to know,* because of what you have to do, is high."

"Are you trying to recruit me, or scare me off?"

"Maybe both. Your father has been working clandestinely with the CIA for the past eight years. He converted to Islam over a decade ago and married a Malaysian woman not long after he divorced your mother."

She stopped in midbite, eyes wide, giving Brock her full attention.

"His wife worked with an import-export company out of Kuala Lumpur, while he wrote inflammatory articles for local papers under an assumed name. He condemned American policies in the Islamic world. His wife had relatives very deep in the radical al-Qaeda sister organization Jemaah Islamiyah."

"Terrorists?"

"To the core. Your father, through one of his wife's cousins, was able to penetrate deeper into this organization than any other agent has in the past. I won't go into details beyond that. All you need to know is that he has in his possession something we desperately need."

It was like being broadsided by hard wind. She had to recover. When she found speech, she asked, for want of a better question while she tried to process the rest of it, "What does he have that's so important?"

"A laptop. It belonged to one of the leaders of Jamaal Islamiyah. We have reason to believe there is information on that laptop of an imminent terrorist mission."

"And he can't get it out?"

"No, he's hurt—"

"How badly?" she asked, interrupting. Panic filled her.

"He was shot in the leg. We don't know more than that."

Her father was hurt. He needed her. Decision made. She'd do whatever she had to, to help her dad.

"Tell me the rest, Brock," she said, leaning back in her seat.

"Most of his network has been killed. He's in hiding on a small island off the coast of Malaysia. He made an attempt to escape, but couldn't make it. There are thousands of tiny islands, some so insignificant they don't even have names. He's on one of them. There are fires on the island and it's under a huge plume of smoke. It's also in the middle of a dangerous area. You'll get a full briefing from CIA when we get to the IC."

"You said that would happen at Miramar. Why should I believe you now that we're on our way to Guam?"

"Sorry about that, but those were my orders. I can tell you this much. An extraction requires a HALO jump into extremely bad conditions on an island controlled at the moment by pirates patrolling the waters and terrorists searching for your father."

A high-altitude, low-opening jump. "And this is something my father thinks only I can do?"

"Apparently that's the case. Yes."

She knew about the incredible fires that were almost yearly events in that part of the world. Thousands of hectares of jungle in the heart of the Malay peninsula, peat-soil fires similar to the fires in Indonesia. The pollutant haze and smoke spread across the entire region all the way to Hong Kong. Most of them were started in land-clearing operations by farmers. They got out of control in the heat of a dry season and just kept burning. Jungle fires have been known to burn for months and months.

She knew that right now over a thousand fires were burning in East Kalimantan province of Indonesia alone. It seemed they would never get a handle on the fires if they couldn't stop farmers from clearing bush for crops and companies from burning forests and jungles after logging to make way for new palm oil plantations. Between the two, the fires came every year. And now, more than a year after the horrible tsunami, and the endless battles with radical guerrilla groups, the fires were burning again.

"You're going to be jumping at night. The fire there is really bad because of all the debris left from last year's tsunami."

"You said I was going to be trained. Trained for what? Jumping I already know."

"Small-arms combat."

He said it as if he was certain she would accept the pronouncement without hesitation. As if packing a gun and having to shoot somebody was just the course of nature…his nature, perhaps, but certainly not hers.

"I'd rather not."

"You can't go into a bad place without some preparation."

"You think you're going to make a soldier out of me overnight?"

"You'd be surprised what I can do with you in a short period of time."

He said it with a blank face, but she peered into those pale green eyes of his and wondered if he was fooling around with a double entendre. She decided he wasn't the type. But then, given her condition, she doubted he was seeing anything to invite double entendres.

"If you can stay awake, I'd like you to practice with a video game." He pulled a laptop from a black case on the floor, opened it and started some sort of combat game. "It's designed to teach the use of small arms in combat situations. You need this training and we don't have a lot of time. You'll need to play various levels of this video game until we get to Guam. Then I'll put you through an intense course until we embark on the mission. It's just a precaution. If things go right, we'll never run into an unfriendly."

"You're jumping in with me?"

"Yes. You can't go in alone. It's too dangerous."

"You're one of those guys."

"What guys?"

"What are they called? Commandos? Special Ops? What are they…oh, right, Delta Force."

Brock concentrated on the video game, not looking at her. Immediately, she knew she'd struck a nerve. Delta Force flew under the radar screen and liked to keep it that way.

"I'm just a soldier on a mission."

Bullshit, she thought. This guy runs around with no uniform, no name tag. Marines are flying him in choppers, then he commands a huge cargo plane with all those other commando-looking guys. Yeah, right, he's just your average soldier. "And I'm a ground-pounding firefighter."

Brock ignored her comment and concentrated on setting up the game.

She asked, "Is this a commercial game?"

"Not quite. This is mine."

"You wrote it?"

"Yes. Military is doing a lot of their own now. It

started with the release of *America's Army* in 2002. That was mostly an interactive army-recruitment ad downloaded by millions of gamers. Since then, they've gotten even more sophisticated."

For once he showed some emotion, some enthusiasm. The guy was human after all.

"This makes better soldiers?"

"Absolutely. Proficiency with the games increases reflex speed to situations, and eliminates thought pauses. Reaction time is everything. The percentage of targets hit has been increasing dramatically per round fired."

"How did you get involved in this? Were you a big game player growing up?"

"Isn't every kid? I was involved for a while in the Army Government Applications office in Cary, North Carolina, with a team of video-game creators and simulation specialists. I worked with guys from Red Storm Entertainment, Interactive Magic, and Timeline. Then I joined another group. This video game isn't for public preview."

"And that's what this is?"

Brock looked as if he was going to smile, like this whole thing turned him on, and he couldn't talk about it enough. She liked him much better like this, but it still didn't mean she trusted the guy.

"Yes. What you'll be dealing with you won't find in your local toy store or video store. This is a big inside industry now. We have a lot of support in the field from several D.C. agencies, West Point and the Special Ops center in Florida where most of the simulation and train-

ing technologies are located. They're all heavily involved in the military-video business."

"They produced this game?"

"It was created by six people. I led the project. You're
going to learn everything you need to know about operating and firing certain weapons under stress. Plus escape and evasion tactics in jungle conditions. We have
games to fit just about every condition, but you'll only
need this one. What's good about this system is I'll
coach and instruct and rerun scenarios until you get
them right. It can condition your reflexes in a few hours
of this kind of prep. Then some fieldwork and in about
the tenth of the time that it used to take, we can have
you online and operational."

He was so convincing that Anna decided to give the
training tool a try, not that she was ready to jump into
a Malaysian warzone, but the game looked interesting
enough.

Anna played war with Brock for six straight hours.
She killed hundreds of people. Some of them over and
over and over until she got it right. He was a very soft-
spoken instructor, nothing like she expected from his
demeanor.

The only weapons Anna had ever fired before were
a shotgun and a hunting rifle. Her mother, an outfitter
in Colorado, was a skeet shooter and a meat hunter.
Neither of those weapons was involved.

At one point when Anna was growing tired of all the
action, she asked, "Do rookie soldiers really learn how
to kill another person by playing these video games?"

"This just helps train reflexes. Gets the brain pathways set. The training's progressive. You'll go out and fire live ammo at shifting targets next. Each step will be faster and closer to the real thing."

She looked at him, trying to get a sense of reality out of him. "You really think you can teach me how to kill someone in a day? Seriously?"

"I can get you close enough that, in a bad situation, you might just react to survive. But it's not a given. Movies and TV shows aside, it's very difficult to turn a civilian into someone who can kill at close range."

"That's comforting."

"Actually, it's true. In fact, studies have shown that soldiers have done all kinds of things to avoid just that. Most ground-combat units in World War I rarely fired their weapons. When they did, they rarely fired to kill. They fired high. Some of them died because they couldn't make themselves kill. Most killing was done from long range. Mortars, bombs, cannon and machine guns. But we've discovered advancements that overcome most of the natural resistance."

"You consider this an advancement?"

"In combat, yes. Not in civilization. I'm not in the business of advancing civilization. I'm in the business of trying to protect it."

"By uncivilized means."

"By any means necessary."

His apparent honesty was about the only thing she liked about him at the moment. "I'm exhausted," she told him after a long yawn. "I've suddenly developed a loathing for this video game and I really don't think you're going to make much of a killer out of me in a hundred days, let alone one. I'd just like to take a nap. There's no shower on this plane, is there?"

"No. You can shower when we get to Guam."

"I can't wait."

He smiled, finally, a warm, charming smile, and she began to warm up to this strait-laced soldier until he said, "Neither can we."

Chapter 4

Anna dreamed that she was naked and clean, lost between creamy white sheets, ecstatic with their cool embrace, but angry at the mattress for being so uncomfortable.

When she woke a second time she still didn't open her eyes. Instead, she listened to the steady drone of the plane's engines, considered getting up, but the thought took too much effort. Weeks of constant grind had taken their toll. It would take a week to recover. Every part of her body ached. She realized she hadn't moved for hours. Her muscles had locked up and she had to work to get them unwound, get some circulation. She stretched one arm, then the other. She finally opened her eyes when a smell wafted to her that she responded to with enthusiasm.

Her body felt like a piece of lead as she undid her seat belt and pulled herself up. The five men on the plane were up front talking and drinking coffee. Three sitting, two standing.

She got up and went forward.

"Coffee's fresh," one of the men said. Brock was talking on a satellite phone.

She accepted the offer of coffee. She smelled of fire and sweat and tried to keep some distance between her smelly self and the men.

After he hung up, Brock brought her a blueberry bagel with cream cheese and another cup of coffee. She was starving again. Then he showed her the island on the computer screen.

They huddled shoulder to shoulder around a laptop and discussed the latest satellite images of the Malaysian and Indonesian fires. The images, acquired by the Moderate-resolution Imaging Spectroradiometer (MODIS) on NASA's Terra satellite, showed a thick soup of smoke.

The island was virtually invisible, covered by a massive cloud of dense smoke.

"Where are the winds?" she asked no one in particular.

"There's no wind. It's dead calm."

Using a new technology she'd never heard of, the images were run though some kind of color spectrometer, and visual penetration became possible. She could see the heat pattern from the fires.

Brock pointed to an area. "This is where we're getting our periodic beeps from. It's the densest and hilliest part of the island. Jason was moving north, but apparently he can't get over those mountains. He's trapped about here," he told her, gesturing to an area.

"How are we getting him out once we get to him?"

"We're hoping to find a burned-over area and bring a chopper in. But the fires are now so big it's getting hard to tell where to land. That's going to be up to you."

She studied the fire pattern, and the distance to the ocean. There were several lagoons, but they had limited information on the island's trees.

"We were thinking of here," Brock said, pointing to a spot. "It's the closest point. The fires aren't joined and that leaves something of an alley."

"No. Too hot." She explained the coloring of the fires. "Whatever the fuel load is in here, it's very hot-burning. Unless you think walking through two thousand degrees won't turn you into a puddle of glue. The best approach is from here." She made a line from one of the lagoons inland. "These must be groves of old hardwood. The fires will be mostly crowning and high. There's a river to the north we can escape to, if things get bad." She pointed to the river. "Once we get to him, I'll find a pickup zone and you can call your guys for a chopper."

While Brock went over plans with his men, she closed her eyes and visualized the jump, the descent, the lagoon where she wanted to go in. Without wind, she'd be able to control the descent, though having to worry about Brock's descent only made hers more risky.

Jumping into a fire from a high altitude at night and into a tropic combat zone was going to be something new. She wasn't at all sure what would happen.

All she wanted to do was just get Brock to the ground and let him take it from there. He's a leader with the most elite commando force on earth, she thought. He should know what he's doing. Just get him in, and he'll get us out.

That's what she hoped for, anyway.

"We'll refuel in the air, put down in Guam in about five hours. If you need more sleep, now's the time."

She walked back to her seat, thinking she might have trouble sleeping again. She cuddled up on her pillow, shut her eyes and immediately floated off into a deep sleep.

Pouco Vulcao Island

Jason Quick came out of a shaking sweat and forced himself to get up. He tried to focus so he could check his symptoms. He feared he was going into some kind of toxic shock syndrome. Septic shock was marked by fever. He had that. Malaise, he had that. Chills and nausea, check. Damn, he was four for four.

He pulled the bandages back and looked at his wound. It was nasty. He cursed bitterly. He had to get the hell off this island and into a hospital, soon.

Jason took a drink from a water bottle, then opened the laptop. He had only two, maybe three hours of battery power left. He closed the computer. He'd been able to translate enough of the text to know what he had, and it was critical he get it out as soon as possible.

Somewhere between Jakarta and Europe a cargo ship had three marine cargo containers with machine tools on board. Inside those machine tools, virtually undetectable by current methods, was enough uranium to make a dozen dirty bombs.

Jason had alerted his handler to the situation a week ago when the containers were first being loaded. It had cost him his cover and the life of his primary agent, a man deep in the terrorist network of Jemaah Islamiyah.

So far nothing had been done to find and stop that ship. But Jason now had a laptop with the information that would identify not only the ship, but where the deadly material was headed. What Jason didn't have was the program that could break the code and get into the specific data on the laptop.

It was his opinion that the cargo was headed for a port in Europe, before heading elsewhere—most likely the States.

He made his way slowly and painfully to the front of the cave. He pushed aside the blanket and stuck his head outside. At times the smoke so completely blocked the sun he couldn't tell if it was day or night but for his watch. The front of the narrow entrance was covered by thick vines and wide lantana fronds. He'd found the cave by accident as he'd fled the men hunting him.

He didn't want to waste the satellite phone's batteries, but he had to make contact. He was getting sicker and weaker by the day. His spells of fever getting worse.

He wouldn't last much longer.

Guam

Anna sensed an absence of movement. They were on the ground.

The door of the transport plane was open, and opening her eyes, she appeared to be alone. They had brought her all the way out to Guam and abandoned her in the plane.

A fine set of circumstances. Her anger and frustration was rising again.

Brock and his associates had, indeed, deplaned without her. No one was on board but her.

She could see the jungle beyond the plane framed in the open door.

Anna unfastened her seat belt, got up and stretched. The heat and light poured in through the open doors with a nasty vengeance.

She deplaned, squinting, and began to sweat almost instantly. It was like walking into a sauna. The sun beat down on her neck and face, the humidity sucked the sweat right up out of her pores onto her skin where it heated up but couldn't evaporate because the air was already saturated. She'd rather be surrounded by fire.

Right across the road from where she stood there was a big sign above the feeder road into the camp: Welcome to Camp Nowhere.

The camp sprawled along the road on the far side of the airfield. No colorful tents like the ones she saw in firefighting camps. This one consisted of a half-dozen Quonset huts with semicircular, corrugated roofs, the structures bolted to large concrete slabs. Behind the Quonset huts stood several smaller stucco buildings and in the distance, across from what looked like a rice paddy, Anna saw several concrete outbuildings.

The sprawling base seemed empty. She had a weird feeling about it, as if she'd stepped into a horror thriller, or one of those great old *Twilight Zone* episodes.

She walked away from the C-17 and then stopped and stood staring across the dirt road at the camp. There was a small road sign: Harm's Way. Hanging from that sign by one arm was a small skeleton of a man that had been fashioned out of wire.

Then, to her right about two hundred yards down the dirt road, barging out of the jungle like a charging rhino, came a Humvee. It careened onto the road, bounced over potholes and headed her way. When it reached the entrance to the airfield it turned toward her and kept on coming as if the driver was going to run her down.

Anna stood her ground, still as a bullfighter awaiting the charge of the bull.

The Humvee came to a skidding halt in a swirl of dust five feet from her.

Brock leaned out the narrow window. "Sleeping Beauty awakens. Hop in, Quick. We have a meeting we're already late for."

Like smoke jumpers, like probably all military-type organizations, last names took precedence over first names. She was Anna to her close friends, Quick to her colleagues. The habit probably came from name tags on military uniforms, last names only.

The doors were off the Humvee, so she wasn't getting into any air-conditioned luxury. Brock wore light-weight tan pants, a green T-shirt and had a weird-looking gun of some kind slung tight next to his chest.

"You going to shoot me?" she asked.

"No. We don't go anywhere without these. I'll get you one after the briefing."

"I can't wait."

She continued to give him a hard look, letting him know she didn't appreciate his exuberance.

In the field about a mile away behind the Quonset huts and other buildings, commandos were drop-roping from two choppers.

She climbed in to the Humvee and they took off toward the camp.

Just then a group of men jogged by in tan shorts and green T-shirts. They all looked the same, as though they were from the same family. A bunch of middleweight fighters, short-cropped hair, hard bodies, all yelling in a sharp cadence.

She began to feel ill, the effects of the heat and the lingering exhaustion.

Too hot.

She had to get the damn fire suit off or she'd pass out. "Can you stop a second?"

He pulled over.

Anna jumped out and unsnapped the suspenders and began pulling the heavy overalls down. She wore black shorts and a gray sleeveless T-shirt underneath.

"Pretty damn hot, isn't it?" Brock said.

She stepped out of the fire suit and tossed it into the back of the Humvee.

"Crazy hot."

"This place is locked and loaded with testosterone," Brock warned. "I wouldn't go any further than that. Where we're going there's air-conditioning."

"I wasn't intending to go any further, at least not until I'm standing in front of a running shower." She refused to get back into the Humvee. "I'm not talking to anybody without a shower and some clean, dry clothes. You've changed clothes, now it's my turn."

Brock chewed on the left part of his bottom lip. He had to think about her attitude for a second. She wasn't in the military so he couldn't call it insubordination. At least not technically. But there was the fact that she'd made that fire jump against direct orders from her boss. So she was insubordinate by nature, apparently.

The thing about her he worked hard to ignore was the shock at how beautiful she was, even under that ash and dirt. It was hard to keep his gaze off her. He turned and looked forward.

"Well, shit," Brock said. "I've got orders to deliver you."

"Why did they send you in the first place? Was it because they knew if they'd sent a CIA guy I wouldn't have believed him for a second without proof?"

"Maybe."

"What if I refuse now?"

"Well, this is a top-secret base and we're in the middle of a global war. I can to shoot you, but then this whole exercise would have been for nothing."

"That's right."

"You're not coming?"

"I'm thinking about it."

Brock looked over at her, frowned and shrugged. "You need a shower and fresh clothes. I can appreciate that."

"That's big of you." She crossed her arms and leaned on one hip. Stubbornness was written all over the woman. He had to quiet the brewing storm.

"Okay, since I'm the one who's going to train you, and jump into this mess with you, we need to get along. So I'll offer a compromise."

She shifted her position. Maybe he was on the right track.

He continued, "This guy we're going to see has a file on your father. We'll be there in about five minutes so he can meet you and know that you're willing to go in. Then, the minute that little bit of time-wasting is over, I'll take you to the showers and get you some clean clothes. Five lousy minutes, that's all I'm asking."

Her arms dropped to her sides. He almost had her. Just a little more reasoning, and she'd see things his way. He was sure of it. "See, the problem is, he's a bureaucrat, CIA type. He runs things on this mission. It's his job to get your father off that island. So, if I were you, and you want to see your dad again, I'd just placate the man for five minutes. Is there any way you can do that for me?"

Anna stared at him for a few seconds. He wasn't

sure which way she would go. Brock hadn't noticed before, but she had the bluest eyes he'd ever seen, and just when he was beginning to believe those eyes were hardening, and he'd have to come up with more bullshit to get her into the Humvee, she climbed in.

It had been a long time since Brock had had to deal with a civilian, or even a regular soldier, for that matter. The kind of men he dealt with were the elite of the elite from all the branches of the military. But he had a feeling that this woman was just as tough.

Anna was too foggy-headed to argue and besides he'd made a compelling case. They passed three more Quonset huts, a couple concrete structures and a few large military tents. She spotted men moving like wolves in the forest that ran alongside the dirt road. Another team of men crossed in front of them and continued into the high grass. These men did have uniforms. Jungle fatigues. And guns.

Brock pulled in front of the end hut.

"Here we are."

"Who's this guy I'm going to meet?" Anna asked.

"Name's Curtis Verrill. He's the head spook around here. This is his mission."

"They run all your missions?"

"No. They often propose. Guys like me, dispose," he said with a smile.

"Meaning that you carry out their orders?"

"Meaning they tell us what they want, and we figure out how to go get it. Could be rescuing somebody, delivering an important package, hunting down a bad guy, whatever."

"In this case recruiting a smoke jumper. Which, I might add, is how this all got started with my father in the first place."

"I don't question the missions, I just figure out how to do 'em. They're the brains, we're the brawn."

"I think you're both. You designed the mission they want done. That takes brains."

He smiled again. "It takes experience and professional common sense."

"Are you modest by nature or by design?"

"Both. I'm a realist. This is an eclectic business. We put together the kind of force structure we need for each job. Each element brings something we need. We live and die by team effort and by always making sure we have the right people for the job."

"Like me?"

"Like you. But not normally. We usually bring in specialists from all branches. Or even go outside the military. Whatever it takes to get the job done. It's like everywhere else. The Ivy League guys dream up something to do, we tell them if it's possible and how to do it. Then we do it and they take all the credit."

She exchanged a little conspiratorial grin with him. She understood perfectly. "A little like having a long discussion on a short topic with Bureau of Land Management people."

He nodded. "You got it. You're about to meet the Bureau of World Management."

"I detect something of a bad attitude."

"My attitude is very flexible," Brock said. "It depends on my proximity to things that irritate me. And right now we're real close to an irritant."

Anna chuckled. As much as she'd have preferred not to like Brock, he was the type, open and self-deprecating, that she could easily connect with.

They got out of the Humvee.

"One more thing," Brock said. "You'll be walking through the communications room on the way back to his office. There aren't any females in there. Or anywhere in the camp, for that matter. Just horny guys who can't get into town. We're in shutdown, mission isolation. Don't even smile. It'll act like a spark in dry hay."

"I'll do my best to ignore anything with more appendages than I have."

"Excuse me, but there's nothing I've seen around here with more appendages than you have. Slump and frown, that might help."

She laughed. What had she gotten herself into?

He pushed open the door and went in ahead of her. She hesitated, staring at him. He turned and shrugged. "I didn't mean to offend."

"You didn't."

Chapter 5

The cool air took her breath away for a moment. The inside of the hut felt just like a refrigerator. She inhaled, as if trying to suffuse every cell with coolness.

There were half a dozen computer workstations, all manned by young men. On the walls, giant maps. Several large printers along the far wall were kicking out page after page of documents. The place hummed with military paperwork.

She and Brock headed to the back as chairs moved and men stepped out of their way.

Not unexpectedly, she actually heard a few very low moans as they walked by. She saw Brock shake his head.

Brock knocked on the only office door in the place. A gruff voice told him to enter. Brock asked Anna to wait.

She stood outside, leaning against the wall, thinking that she needed to call her mother at some point and explain where she was and to tell her that her father was alive. Her mom was going to be shocked. Anna didn't know the protocol on this CIA base and didn't want to do anything stupid. Her dad's life was in danger and she didn't want to be the one to end it—just by making a phone call. Her mother was probably out in the mountains with her satellite phone, so it wouldn't be difficult to contact her. But should she? They usually talked three or four times a week, sharing adventure stories. This time, she'd have more to share than a fire adventure. This time she would raise the dead. She had a feeling her mother wouldn't believe it, and at that precise moment, Anna could barely believe it herself. But if she didn't call, her mom would worry. Anna didn't want that.

About ten minutes later, while Anna had fallen into memories of her dad, Brock opened the door and motioned her inside.

The stern-looking man sitting behind the desk told her to have a seat. "I'm Curtis Verrill," he said without looking up from a file he was leafing through. Like that was more important at this moment than making eye contact. She knew right off that she wasn't going to like this guy.

Verrill wore tan khakis and a blue short-sleeved knit shirt with no insignia. After a few moments, he finally sat back, looked up and studied Anna for a second.

He said, "I apologize for all the secrecy and hassle. Believe me, this has been as difficult for us as it has been for you."

"And why is that?"

He didn't appear to like the question, or maybe the tone, so he ignored it. "We have a problem—"

"And I take it, I'm the solution."

He didn't respond to that either, but he did throw an accusatory look at Brock, as if to say he knew where her prejudgment had come from.

He picked up a brown folder and held it in his left hand. "Your father's files. I'm sure you have some questions."

She stared at the folder. After all these years CIA was suddenly going to tell her the truth about her father's disappearance.

She reached across the desk for the folder, but he pulled it back. Apparently, he wasn't *really* going to tell her anything. Now she really didn't like the man.

Verrill related the reasons her father went under, the reasons for the cover story, his extreme value as an agent. "For an American to have any credibility in a Muslim culture, he has to be one of them. Marry into their world. Live, dress, eat and sleep like they do for a long period of time. Do business. Have a solid bona fide relationship with the people around him. Your father succeeded in all of that. He was well known and well accepted. Once he was in, he began to network."

She listened to the story and wondered if it was any truer than what she'd believed about her father before. These people were professional deceivers. He wouldn't have put his own daughter through all that sorrow and pain for a job, even if it was for national security. He would have found some way to contact her. To let her know he was still out there. Alive.

Brock had already told her most of what Verrill was saying about the mission. Everyone, she was sure, was well versed in this story, but no one seemed to have a good reason about her father wanting her to come in after him.

"Why me?"

"I can't answer that," Verrill admitted. "We have the highest qualified smoke jumpers in the world. We didn't need to go to a...civilian."

You left a word out, Anna thought, but what was it? Female, perhaps?

She felt a little like she'd taken a wrong step and had fallen into the rabbit hole, Alice in Jungleland. She was standing there in the middle of the Pacific with this CIA agent and this Special Ops guy telling her she was going to jump onto some tiny island—an island in the middle of the pirate and terrorist country—in less than twenty-four hours to rescue her father.

It seemed completely unbelievable to her.

There had been times when smoke jumping felt the same way. She went from putting out one small fire to the next, and the next, and after about five or six of them she no longer could think straight.

Perhaps this was one of those times.

"If this is all true, why wouldn't he have contacted us? We thought he was dead."

"He couldn't contact you. Not you, his ex-wife, rel-atives or friends because that's the nature of the business he's in. He took on a different name, different identity. He had to be believed. Any suspicions might have put you and your mother in jeopardy."

* Verrill handed her a photograph. "This was taken two months ago."

The man in the photo was getting out of a car, wearing Muslim headgear and clothing, deeply tanned, older, but it was her dad. The nose, the shape of the face. Definitely him.

Then Verrill started lecturing her on how critical the mission was, how important it was to get her father out. That the free world was depending on her. He called it Operation Fierce Snake.

She stared at Verrill, but her mind was on her father and that day he'd left and never returned. She remembered him turning as he was getting into a friend's car. She was getting ready to go to her first year at the University of Colorado. He'd winked, smiled and said, "Be good. Be quick."

She had laughed. "We have to live up to our name."

He'd smiled and given her a thumbs-up.

According to Brock, her dad was already remarried by then. He'd never said a thing.

Then Verrill regained her attention. "We're still getting some weak, random signals from his locator. He's up on the mountain. He has some contacts on the island and one of them will meet you when you go in. Brock will fill you in on the details."

Her father had divorced her mother twelve years ago, but he never talked about it, or berated her mother. She'd been one of those very lucky girls to have the greatest of fathers. Anna knew, and apparently so did the CIA, that she'd go anywhere, risk anything, to get him back.

Verrill continued, "Malaysia is off-limits. If you go in, I don't know anything about it. If you don't come out, I know nothing about that either."

Anna glanced at Brock. He was impassive.

Verrill said, "You will go into training immediately and train continuously until you leave. That's all."

He stood now and reached out to shake her hand. She shook it, but somehow she knew it was simply a formality. There was nothing friendly about the gesture. "Good luck," he said, and pulled his hand back.

The way he said it, the dark flicker in his eyes, sent a chill through Anna. She knew he really didn't believe she could get in there and get her father out.

She'd prove him wrong.

She followed Brock out of the office, through the Quonset hut and back into the heat.

"I would like to call my mother in Colorado."

"No problem. But you can't tell her anything about your father or what you're up to. You should call her soon, because once we start the training you won't have time to talk to her until after we get back. Plus, you should know that any calls going out of here will be monitored."

A man coming out of one of the other Quonset huts walked toward them. He had the confident swagger of someone born and bred to run things, as comfortable at the country club as on a secret military base. "Anna

Quick, I'm Tom Roca." He shook hands with her. "Welcome on board. I heard about your saving those college kids. That was very fine work."

She nodded. "Thanks."

"Take good care of her, Brock," Roca said, his eyes shifting for a brief second to Brock.

Brock didn't answer.

"Great to meet Jason Quick's daughter," Roca said. "Enjoy your training." He gave her a little smile, then walked into Verrill's hut.

When he was gone, Anna turned to Brock as she climbed into the Humvee. "A friend of yours?"

"Not exactly. CIA. One of Verrill's boys. Actually, he thinks he's running this mission," Brock said sardonically. "Practice before he assumes the job of running the universe."

Anna smiled. She was starting to like Brock more and more.

They drove on to the village of Quonset huts down the road. She reflected on the tension between Roca and Brock, and Brock's attitude toward Verrill. Not a happy group. She wondered what had happened to cause such hostility between them, and hoped it wouldn't affect their chances of a successful operation.

Anna called her mom on a Sat phone Brock gave her—one, no doubt, that scrambled the conversation and made it impossible to be intercepted and decoded. She assured her mom that she was all right and was just going to sleep in for the next few days. Then she finally took a shower. She lingered in the downpour like a starved desert plant under the season's first rain. She didn't care if she used up all the water on the base, she was going to get clean. There were times, and this was one of them, when a shower or bath vaulted ahead of food, shopping or sex as life's great relaxer. She didn't need yoga, prayer, drugs or alcohol to get centered. She just needed water and soap.

Brock had gone somewhere to get her some clothes. When he came back she heard him on the other side of the door. "Everything you need is here."

"Thanks."

Fatigue breaks down the walls of reason and lets in unbidden thoughts, such as she was naked and a foot away was a handsome soldier. She smiled at her erotic nonsense. She wished she had time for a longer daydream but she was sure Brock was pacing outside, waiting for her to finish.

After the shower she found a pile of clothes just outside the stall on a chair. A green T-shirt, light nylon pants with four side pockets and jungle sneakers. High-fashion commando gear.

"Quick, you dressed?" Brock yelled from somewhere outside.

"Yes," she called out. He walked in sooner than she'd expected, so she turned her back to him while she pulled her shirt down.

"Shower feel good?" Brock asked.

"I'm almost human."

"You get that scar jumping?"

Shit.

She hated that he saw the scar on her back. She'd been planning on getting some skin grafts to get rid of it, but hadn't had the time. "Yeah. Hit a snag. I didn't have body armor on. It's ugly, I know. I'm going to get it fixed one of these days."

"It's your badge of courage," he protested.

"I like badges I can hide away in the drawer."

He laughed and pulled up his shirt to display two nasty scars on his stomach. "Like these."

The scars were there, but she was seeing the body that was holding them in place. The man had no fat on him. Didn't she see a book in Barnes & Noble once with some title about the diet of the warrior among the thousand or so other diet books? Brock could be the cover.

She asked, trying to be nonchalant, "How did you get those?"

"Some moron tried to blow up a convoy I was hitching a ride on. Long story, bad ending for a lot of good people." He tucked in his shirt. "Don't think of a scar you earned in battle as ugly. There's nothing ugly about it."

She wasn't going to argue with him, serious as he was. Especially when his scars represented something very emotional and deep. But she fully intended to get rid of hers…one of these days.

She followed him out to the Humvee and jumped into the passenger seat.

Anna rubbed her eyes. "The training for all of this had better be good."

He gave her a wry glance, then headed down the road.

When they'd gone a few hundred yards, he said, "We'll get in about a thousand rounds."

"What? I need that much?"

"It's my job to prepare you the best I can. Besides, if you're with me I want to know I've made you very comfortable with Heckler and Koch."

"Who are they?"

"They are the assault weapons you'll be married to until we're extracted. A thousand rounds from now you'll think you were born with them in your hands."

"I'm so excited," she said sarcastically. "How long does it usually take to train somebody for your line of work?"

"Couple years. Couple million rounds."

"I'm going to be proficient with Heckler and Koch in a day? Yeah, right."

"*Familiar* is the operative word. Proficient is a marriage of talent and practice we don't have the time for. Just give it a chance, okay?"

She nodded.

They rode in silence for a time, then Brock glanced over at her. "You may or may not hit the bad guys. I just want to make sure you don't shoot me should a crisis arise."

Excuse me, she thought with an inner smile, but you, my friend, are way too necessary to my survival to shoot. "I'll try not to."

"What's between you and the CIA?" Brock asked.

"Years of lies."

"Then it must feel good to finally know the truth."

"Is it?"

"You don't believe that your father is alive?" He glanced over at her, a look of confusion on his face.

"I don't know yet," she explained. "I guess I do. It's just such a shock, it's hard to bring this whole thing into focus. If he's really in trouble, I want to get him out of there. Once he's safe, then I'll go ahead and have whatever kind of joyful nervous breakdown it requires."

"We'll get him out," Brock said. "Given your record and mine, I'd say as a team we might just be the best there is at extracting somebody from a very bad situation."

Flattery no less. She wondered what the structure of his thought patterns might be. He never appeared condescending, like Verrill, which she found to be a bit of a shock. He didn't seem to possess any really annoying macho mannerisms toward her. Anna had run into just about every variety of male as a smoke jumper. The heroes and the assholes. She was sure the military was no different. Brock was a mystery that didn't look to be easy to unravel. He was charming, no doubt about that, but charm could be the most venomous of snakes. It always put women in a weak position. Anna liked to know who her friends and enemies were up front and the charmer never allowed that. They were the real high-stakes poker players in the game. The ones she had to look out for.

Another group of men appeared out of the jungle and jogged in single file across the road in front of them. These men wore jungle camouflage, carried weapons and had blackened faces. Brock slowed to let them get across the road and into the high grasses of the field.

"Why haven't any females broken through this elite barrier yet?"

He gave her a sidelong glance with that enigmatic half smile of his.

"They have now."

Watch this guy closely, Anna thought. He's saying all the right things.

She was in trouble.

Chapter 6

Bethesda, Maryland

Stanford Ellis watched the silver-haired jogger move at a loping gait along the Potomac River until he turned off the trail and settled into a fast walk.

The jogger, Frank Patterson, was searching for Ellis, finally spotting him in a tree grove. He looked around as if making sure they were alone, then walked over to his former boss.

"Where are we?" Ellis asked.

"Verrill's assembling a team to go in."

"They still getting response from Jason Quick?"

"Yeah."

"Who's going in?"

"Quick's daughter, Anna. She's a smoke jumper and he's demanding she come in with the team."

"What!"

"I don't know what the hell's going on with him. Verrill says Quick is over the edge. Full-blown paranoia. He won't cooperate unless we send his daughter in. She's agreed. We pulled her off a fire in California."

Patterson shrugged, then shook his head. He was a CIA agent who'd worked for nine years under Ellis before Ellis was pushed out. "John Brock, Special Ops, took her to Guam for some quick OJT to get her ready to jump on that island."

"Quick wants his daughter in that mess? He must be crazy."

"It's bizarre as hell. Verrill thinks he's farther over the edge than we first thought."

"I can't believe she agreed."

"Well, she's at the Guam IC right now. Verrill's not happy about sending anybody in there. It's a miserable situation. The island is on fire. It's a real no-man's-land. Neither Malaysia nor Indonesia have any authority in that area. Thousands of little islands. Most of them either controlled by pirates or criminal enterprises. Or Jemaah Islamiyah terrorists. Verrill thinks maybe the best way to play this—"

"I don't give a rat's ass about Verrill's worries. We need to get rid of this bastard and get that damn laptop. Verrill understands that his name might be on one of those files, doesn't he?"

"Yeah. But he thinks if we play it so we can't find Quick, he'll just die on his own."

"So he thinks."

"Or somebody from the Jemaah Islamiyah will get to him if he's out there long enough."

"Can't risk it. The laptop is still out there. Besides, it's too late for that. We have to make sure this is buried and buried deep."

"The ship's on course to arrive in three days in Marseilles."

"Then you tell Verrill he better get moving."

Patterson sucked in his breath, and said, "Consider it done."

"Failure is not an option."

Patterson nodded. He turned and retraced his steps along the trail.

Ellis watched him go, then he took out his cell phone and made a call.

"Operation Blowback is green."

The voice on the other end said, "Good."

After he hung up, Ellis started back toward his estate a half mile away. A pair of good-looking women in their early twenties jogged by in their tiny shorts and sports bras, jabbering away.

Neither of them noticed him. He couldn't get used to that. He no longer had power. That would soon change. Stanford Ellis's gaze followed them with an intense melancholy until they vanished.

A deep anger smoldered within him. He'd been betrayed and shoved aside by the very government he'd given his whole life to, but he was far from out of the game.

Blowback was a term Ellis had coined decades ago. It referred to the effect of past operations and, often, mistakes on the present policy and missions. Now everybody in the CIA used the term. There was a certain sweet irony in naming his mission Operation Blowback.

Stanford Ellis no longer hated the idea of aiding and abetting the terrorists. That was just tactical. The real enemy was in Washington, D.C.

The fat cats needed to be punished and Ellis would be more than happy to see them get it.

He despised their arrogance.

In the end, they'd be begging him to come back, to save them.

There was only one man who could hurt Blowback. He was already half-dead on some damn island in the Strait of Malacca. But half-dead wasn't good enough.

If Quick wanted his daughter to become collateral damage, to go down with him, that was too bad.

It's all about sacrifices, Ellis reflected somberly. Every important juncture in history demands sacrifices.

Part Two
Warrior

Chapter 7

Guam

They drove in complete silence along the rough dirt road, the sun blazing down on them. Brock was keeping something tight to his chest, but Anna had a pretty good idea what it might be. She glanced at him as they neared the training camp. "You really hate bringing me into this, don't you?"

"I follow orders," he said with resolute conviction.

Anna stared at him for a moment, trying to get a fix on what was going through the man's head. She had a feeling it had to do with her last jump and the fact that she'd disregarded her orders. "You're a soldier and soldiers take orders even if they don't like them, right?"

"That's right."

"I didn't ask for this, you know."

"No, your father did."

"So, let's just deal with it the best we can."

He didn't reply. Instead, he gave her a sidelong glance, then turned back to the road. "Look, I don't take civilians on operations. Especially on operations like this. It's stupid."

"And female ones at that."

"You can't push that button with me. I have nothing against trained female soldiers who follow orders. This operation is just you and me. We're not going in with a whole team. So, no, I don't like it. I don't like the way it's set up, the way it's going to be executed—I don't like anything about it. But your father has a lot to do with that. He's the one who's calling the shots."

"And he's CIA?"

"That's right. And you're his daughter. But don't let my concerns bother you. I'll do my job."

Okay, Anna thought, at least he's pretty straightforward even if he's going to make my life difficult.

She had to agree that this was a dangerous and unusual operation, but she wasn't that far yet with her emotions. She was still struggling with the enormity of the idea that her father was actually alive, hiding on an island, wounded and waiting for her to come in and get him.

Of course, she was thrilled that he was alive, but she

was also angry that he'd married and never told her, that he'd deserted her.

Anna turned to Brock. She wanted to keep a rapport with this guy, even if it was somewhat strained. "Have you been in Malaysia on operations before?"

Brock nodded.

When he didn't say anything, she asked him what they were about and he said curtly, "The past is something an operator doesn't discuss. You'd be wasting your time asking any of us about anything but the current problem."

"That's what you call yourselves, operators?"

"That's what we are. And for the time being, that's what you are."

She thought the term was unsuited to what these shadow warriors, these modern commandos, were doing. It sounded like they worked for a phone company rather that the U.S. government.

Brock turned into the main section of the encampment and approached a group of rounded metal Quonset huts. They looked like giant tin cans cut in half and randomly dropped into a rice field. The two concrete buildings across the street seemed out of place in this tin world.

He parked in front of one of the huts but didn't get out. Anna sat tight, waiting to see what he was going to do next. He turned toward her, resting his hand on the steering wheel.

"I've worked with your father indirectly. I knew him by a code name and got to know more about him than

I probably should have. He's a good man, but I can't tell you any more than that. I'm sure there's a good reason why he wants you to come in with me, but, the truth is—" he shook his head "—I don't understand why he'd put you through all of this. He must have a damn good reason. But that's not my concern. I have a job to do and it's my duty to follow through, no matter what I think about it."

"Thank you."

"It's not personal. It's my job."

A good soldier's soldier. Mission focused. "You've worked with Verrill before?" she asked.

"In the theater. Sometimes I'm not sure of anything but the particular operation. The less we know, the less an enemy can find out in the event of our capture."

That wasn't a pleasant notion. She tried to imagine what it would be like to get captured by terrorists, getting beaten, raped, tortured and beheaded. "I think I'd rather be killed than captured," she admitted.

Brock looked off in the distance for a moment, his expression intense. "Sometimes you don't have the opportunity to get yourself killed. You're wounded or ambushed so suddenly you have no defense against capture. Which is all the more reason why I'm going to run you through the training program on a fast track. Get you as familiarized with the equipment as I can. You *will* know how to use small arms before this day is out."

"I can't wait," she said with a mild hint of sarcasm.

Anna followed Brock into one of the metal huts. It was obviously a supply hut, filled with racks of equipment, clothes and weapons. "That's your stuff," he said, pointing to gear and guns on one of the tables.

Brock handed her a helmet with a night-vision goggle attached. "It's voice activated. Has enhanced hearing capability. Kevlar Nomex mix. Everything we are going in with has been designed precisely for this type of operation. It's light, fire retardant, the pockets and backpack waterproof."

"You guys have tech support who create what you need, like James Bond?"

"Something like that," he said with a laugh.

He handed her a gun, holding it in his hands as if he was handling a piece of fine china. "This is the MP-5K submachine gun. You can take this—" he picked up another gun, short, odd-looking weapon "—or this." It had a weird shape. The gun was unlike anything she'd ever seen before. "It's a fully dressed P-90 Personal Defense weapon. Less than twenty inches long and six and a half pounds."

She held one, then the other.

Brock worked the action on them. "Both are weapons of choice for jumping into tight areas like jungles. The P-90 is about as wide as my body across the chest. You can run around in the jungle and not snag things."

"I've never seen a gun like this."

"The P-90 is pretty new. You'll probably like it. A lot of Europeans are using it. It has a flatter trajectory than conventional open-bolt submachine guns and that makes it more accurate." He pointed to the end of the barrel. "This is the flash suppressor. It carries a 50-round horizontal magazine that lies on top." He snapped off a see-through clip. "And, as you can see, the bullets are visible so you know how many rounds are left. Because it doesn't stick down, like most magazines, you can lie prone and not have to turn on your side to pull out the mag and reload. You just snap this baby off and seat another in, never changing positions. We'll try them both and you can choose."

Half of what he said went over her head. All she needed was a weapon that would keep her alive. "I like the feel of this one," she said of the MP-5K. She wasn't sure if she'd said it because she actually liked the feel better, or just to be contrary.

"Shoot both. Then decide."

Next, Brock showed her a fighting knife and then a 9 mm handgun. He explained that it was a Glock with a quick-release rig that was worn on the thigh.

Anna pulled the pistol from its holster. "I'm going to learn how to be proficient with all this stuff in one day?"

"I can't promise that you'll be proficient." Brock secured the holster around her thigh and adjusted it to fit. The feel of his hands on her leg sent a jolt up her body that she was unprepared for. "But you will be familiar. That's a good first step." He removed the holster, apparently satisfied that it fit. "Let's try the suit on. We're going in as light as we possibly can. Once on the ground, we'll be slogging through jungle and forest, climbing, maybe running. The outfit needs to be right. These suits are still experimental. Nothing like them is out on the market yet. You're used to carrying in about forty pounds on a fire jump, aren't you?"

"Yes. But coming out, it's a lot more."

"Why's that?"

"The pickup point is sometimes miles away, and we carry out all the equipment dropped in to fight the fire. Like chain saws. They're heavy. I've come out with over a hundred pounds on my back, slogging up and down hills for miles after days of digging trenches, cutting trees and setting backfires, so I'm used to carrying weight."

She took the suit from him, felt the fabric and the lightness. Amazing material.

He said, "Then this will be a cinch for you. Let me show you how to gear up."

She was used to having team members check each other's equipment and adjust backpacks, but this outfit had belts everywhere and he was, necessarily, all over her. She showed no reaction to the intimacy of his hands, but couldn't help noticing how hard he seemed to be working to keep himself in a clinical mode, careful, gentle and matter-of-fact, talking the whole time about where she'd put tape to cover metal, that it was fireproof tape. He was proud of the equipment.

He showed her the fastest way in and out of her body armor, web belts, knee pads, drop-down holster and the operation of the Harris digital radio. He explained that the Molle patrol pack had been redesigned and would carry everything she needed for the mission. He handed her a jump M3T helmet, specially equipped with a boom and microphone mount, detachable goggles and a night-vision monocular mount. She slipped it on her head, and it fit perfectly, feeling lighter than her own jump helmet.

With all of her new gear on, she could move freely. "It's great not to have to duck-waddle like we do in our jumpsuits." She walked back and forth, squatting, testing flexibility. It was almost the same as wearing street clothes.

"No military on earth can match this outfit." Brock said, sounding a little like a salesman.

"I'm impressed. Everything seems to fit," she said.

He nodded, and smiled a little, as if he was proud of his accomplishments so far. "Looks good."

She decided Brock was a man, programmed for low tolerances and high efficiency. It gave her a sense of comfort knowing she was going in with somebody like him. It was how she saw herself as a firefighter. Once the gear was on, and the plane in the air, it was all business.

As they were leaving the hut to get something to eat before heading to the range, she said, "I think we'll do okay."

He smiled nodded. "I'm sure we will."

Walking out of the metal building with a gun on her hip and another slung across her chest felt odd. She always thought of herself as someone who saved lives, not someone who took them. It was a strange feeling knowing she might have to turn that philosophy on its head.

"You have a good relationship with your father growing up?" Brock asked.

The question surprised her. "Yes. I worshiped my father," she answered as they headed toward the mess hall.

"Go on ahead, get whatever you want," he said. "I'll be there in a few minutes. I need to get a couple of things. I'll brief you on some more facts about the specifics of the mission, then we'll go shoot."

Anna crossed the road and walked toward one of the concrete buildings that Brock had pointed to.

Brock watched her until she disappeared inside the building. Out of the corner of his eye he saw a couple of his team members heading his way. They, no doubt, wanted a report.

"So that's the fire jumper," Swartzlander muttered sarcastically. "Looks like a tight package."

Brock nodded. He knew what was coming.

"You make a soldier out of her yet?" DeAngelo asked.

"Smoke jumpers are soldiers," Brock shot back, feeling a need to defend his charge in spite of his feelings. "All I can do is show her how to use different tools. What's the update?" he asked DeAngelo.

"The ship's late in getting into the Strait. A couple hundred miles to get it into place. Weather's not cooperating. I don't think it'll be a go tonight."

The ship was a freighter that had been converted for Special Operations. From the outside it would look like every other freighter carrying goods through the pirate-infested Strait of Malacca—the five-hundred-mile corridor between Malaysia and Indonesia that linked the shipping routes from the South China Sea to the Indian Ocean—but it was all American military on the inside.

"We getting anything from the island?" Brock asked Swartzlander.

"Weak signal every few hours. He's not risking anything. Must have low batteries. Or they're dead. We can't get a call to him. Just the locator."

Brock nodded. Another day would be pushing it. "We getting any new traffic from Jimmy Jihad?"

Swartzlander said, "We're getting lots of traffic. They appear to have about six teams working the island in grids. Moving very slow and careful inland towards the hills. They seem to think he's hiding somewhere in a cave or in one of the remote villages."

The island, called Pouco Vulcao, little volcano, had been hit hard by the '04 tsunami and had never recovered. Now it was burning. The island was at the outer edge of thousands of tiny islands that were home to radical jihadists, pirates and organized-crime syndicates that preyed on shipping. With the massive international effort to freeze financial assets, terrorist groups had turned to piracy as a source of funding in the area. Almost half of all piracy attacks in the world took place in Strait of Malacca.

"Fighting fires and fighting guerrilla terrorists are two different things," Swartzlander said. "You really think you can make a one-day wonder out of her?"

"It's the mission they gave me."

The thing about Swartzlander was he had all sorts of opinions he felt everybody had a right to hear whether they liked it or not. Brock ignored him most of the time.

"I'm just damn glad it's not me," Swartzlander said. "I never want to back out of a mission, but this one might have put that to the test. PC bullshit aside—"

"Nobody cares about your would-haves," Brock snapped.

"—there's no way in hell I'd want to drop in that bad-ass place with any female. I don't care if she's the meanest, nastiest Amazon dyke on earth. No way. But a civilian? No way. Some of these spooks are missing some screws."

Brock had been wrong enough times about female soldiers in the past to refrain from a locked-down position until the evidence proved one way or another. Swartzlander and DeAngelo were both looking at him for his opinion.

"She's a required asset in this operation," he told them. "I have no choice. But I'll tell you one thing, I watched her make a jump into the biggest, ugliest fire I've ever been in close contact with. A jump no sane person would make and none of her comrades were willing to make. She saved four college kids from certain death. Dug in and rode out the fire. And I know she's also a strong woman, capable of hauling out a hundred pounds of gear after fighting a fire up and down hills all damn day long. Guts and stamina aren't bad ingredients. I wouldn't want to jump onto that burning island with anybody else."

He hadn't really thought about it before, but after he'd said it, he realized it was true. Maybe Jason Quick knew what he was doing after all.

"They aren't the things that count in a firefight with pirates and terrorists, and that island is full of them," Swartzlander argued.

"Not a hell of a lot I can do about it, is there?"

"You going to introduce us, right?" DeAngeleo asked.

"In passing. You shell casings can pay your respects. Anything beyond that is out of order." Brock gave Swartzlander a look to let him know he wasn't kidding.

Their low rumblings rolled easily across the quiet grounds of the vast compound as the three of them headed for the mess hall.

Pouco Vulcao Island

Sweat rolled down Jason Quick's face and into his eyes. He squinted and rubbed his burning eyes, trying to get them to clear. He'd fallen off his cot swinging at big rats that were nibbling on his toes. He fired his gun into the corner as they scurried away. "C'mon you bastards, c'mon!"

He felt an ice block in his stomach, cold and painful, as he wiped away the sweat.

Water. He needed water.

He found the water bottle under the cot and drank until he felt satisfied. Then he tried to sit up, to get up, but the weakness spread across him like cement, holding him down.

He told himself to be still a moment. To get centered, grounded. He prayed to Allah, to God.

I can't go into shock. I can't...

He saw her, his wife, drifting lightly through the palms near the edge of the beach, walking as if not touching the ground at all, so fluid, like beautiful water, smiling, eyes full of joy. And his boys. They stop and turn to the strangest sight, the sea receding. Her eyes lose their joy, replaced now by something. What? A piece of knowledge, a bit of information long ago learned. She's alarmed and runs to her boys...

Jason turned over and opened his eyes. He bumped

the table, and the oil lamp moved, sending shadows dancing wildly on the cave ceiling and walls.

He struggled to get himself back up on the raised mats. It was an exhausting effort. He put the small automatic pistol beside the bed and lay down, sweating and staring at the jagged walls.

"Azalina! Where are you? Azalina!"

Chapter 8

Guam

When Anna walked into the mess hall there were about fifteen men sitting around at various tables, eating, talking, laughing. She got a few blank looks, but then nothing but the cold shoulder.

The soldiers ignored her as she went to the mess line and got herself the day's chow: rolls, beef stew, green beans, potatoes and black coffee.

She sat at a table by herself.

Okay, she thought, don't even look at the new girl on base. Anna was amused by what she perceived as a hostile reception in the mess hall. She'd been through this so many times in the past with smoke jumping it was impossible to be disturbed by it. They'd adjust. Besides, she wouldn't be hanging around that long. They'd get over it.

Anna was about to start eating, when Brock came in with a couple of men. They walked over and Brock introduced her to a dark-complexioned guy named Swartzlander, who gave her a rattlesnake stare, and DeAngelo, a redhead who looked as if he wanted to sit, have a beer and get to know her. That didn't happen. Instead, the two men moved to the food line and didn't return.

"They part of your team?"

"Yeah," Brock said. He went and got himself a cup of coffee, then came back and sat across from her at the table.

She glanced around. "How do you get to be Special Ops?"

"Operators come from many backgrounds—Special Forces, Air Recon, Navy SEALs. The guys at the far table are Military Intelligence. Those two by the wall are CIA."

Anna watched small groups of men come and go. Many of them would give her a brief glance, then go about their business in this shadowy world of clandestine global operations. The warriors. Behind the mystery and the mystique, these guys, with one or two exceptions, looked so ordinary it was hard to imagine them as the point of the spear, the hunter-killers in the war on terror. Yet that was what they were.

Brock drank his coffee slowly as he looked at some notes he had. Then he reached into his right-side cargo pocket and came up with a map. He put it on the table. Anna wondered about his background, how he got to be the leader of a team. She didn't even know what rank he held.

Brock finally focused on her. "You were a big-time soccer player at the University of Colorado?"

They probably knew when she uttered her first burp at birth. "I played with the University of Colorado Women's Soccer Club."

"I heard you were pretty good. That your team was the best in the country."

"The Colorado Gold won four National Championship games. I was in the 2001 game."

"That's impressive."

"Colorado Gold was the only team to make it into the final rounds for eleven straight years."

"You ever think of going pro?"

"I entertained the idea for a while," she said. "Then I got some pins inserted in my ankle and knee after a bad fall, that pretty much put an end to that."

"That's too bad. Maybe you would have been the next Mia Hamm."

"I don't know about that. But I'm a big believer in things happening for a reason."

"I wish I was," Brock said. "I've seen too many things that happen for no damn good reason at all."

She liked that they were having a real conversation. "How long have you been in the military?"

Brock held his coffee just below his mouth, pausing, "Going on eleven years."

"I guess you're going the whole way?"

He took a drink and put the cup down on the table between them.

"At least twenty. Unless they buy me out before then."

"Who's *they?*"

"There's a lot of private money looking for guys from my world. Our stock is sky-high right now."

"Corporations?"

"Corporations, politicians, Vegas casinos, foreign hostage rescue, private global security firms. There's employment blossoming all over the globe. We have all kinds of options and that's hurting us. Guys with experience get offered so much money it's getting hard to hold on to them just when we need them the most."

He was finally opening up to her and she wanted to keep the momentum going.

"How many people are we talking about?"

"Total package? Around the globe? About fifty thousand. One of my mentors is now an analyst on CNN. Everybody is looking to buy us out."

They were silent for a minute. Then she said, "You have family?"

"A brother who's a lawyer in Baltimore. Parents in Kansas City."

"Wife?"

"Ex."

"Kids?"

"No." And he said it in a way that was like a hammer coming down on that line of questioning. It put an end to the mutual-discovery chitchat altogether.

Okay then, she reasoned. The wife-and-family story wasn't up for discussion.

Anna finished her beef stew, or whatever the meat-like substance was, and started feeling tired again. She sure could use another ten hours, but that fantasy was never going to happen, so she took a deep breath, and went for another cup of coffee.

When she returned, Brock turned the map so she could see it. "This is our destination." He pointed to a long stretch of water that slanted off the Malay Peninsula. Borneo lay to the east in the South China Sea. At the bottom of the map, off the tip of Sumatra, lay Java. The whole area was divided between Indonesia and Malaysia. "Right here," he said as he pointed to the long channel between Sumatra and the Malay Peninsula, "is the Strait of Malacca. There are seventeen thousand islands, and every day a quarter of world trade, half of all oil shipments bound for eastern Asia and two-thirds of global shipments of liquefied natural gas go through this strait. Which is a gauntlet. The most dangerous place for the global economy. Your father helped design and update a two-hundred-year-old model for securing this area. That model was the war on piracy we fought against Mediterranean pirates on the Barbary Coast."

"I never heard of the Strait of Malacca before."

"The media isn't interested. Yet. It's not important enough. But today's pirates use modern equipment, automatic weapons, antitank missiles, satellite phones, global positioning systems, and they're trained with military precision. And increasingly, they're being taken over by radical terrorist organizations linked to al-Qaeda. In this case it's Jemaah Islamiyah. The threat to Malacca shipping has increased and now they're going after oil tankers. It's all part of a program by terrorist groups to get a real maritime capacity. Not just speed-boats packed with explosives to ram ships like the *USS Cole* back in 2000. Or the French oil tanker *Limburg*. They have much bigger things in mind. First they start with phantom ships that they hijacked. These are re-painted, named and registered under flags-for-hire places like Liberia, Malta and Panama."

"Can't we stop this?"

"Apparently not," he said. "Indonesia and Malaysia can't patrol the strait or the seventeen thousand-plus islands, yet they don't want America or anyone else to do it. A catastrophic disruption of world energy by terror-ists has been in the making for years and people like your father are on the frontlines trying to stop it. But that isn't our concern at the moment."

He folded up the map and put it back in his cargo pocket. "We have reason to believe there's a ship with something nasty on board that's headed for a port, pos-sibly in Europe before changing ships and heading for the States. Only we don't know what ship or what port. The laptop that your father has contains the information about this ship. That's why he's being hunted by the Jemaah Islamiyah. And that's why we need to get to him first. He's been on the run for almost a week, and as I said he's been wounded. We don't know how much longer he can survive. That's the long and the short of it. We need to get him and that laptop out of there. Hopefully in time to stop that cargo ship."

She envisioned her dad, wounded and on the run. If she could, she'd leave for the island right now. All she wanted to do was get him out of there.

"You said you've worked with him in the past?"

"Yes, because of situations involving some hijackings in that arena."

Anna had little problem believing this was the alternative life her father lived. He was a man who had always loved adventure. The more dangerous, the better. "My father must be very good at what he does."

"He's the only penetration we've ever gotten into some of the organizations like the Free Aceh Movement, an Indonesian separatist group that was trying to launch attacks on Malacca shipping just last year. They are experts at hijacking ships and taking their crews hostage. He was also instrumental in getting information on the Tamil Tiger separatists who carried out suicide attacks on five boats and an oil tanker off northern Sri Lanka. Your father got himself embedded with these widespread terrorist organizations partly through marriage. After he lost his family in the tsunami—"

"What?"

"Your father had a Malaysian family and he lost them in that catastrophe."

Anna was stunned. Before, he'd only mentioned another wife... "What family?"

"Two sons and a daughter. His wife was also killed."

All those hours of watching the horror of that catastrophe on TV and never once could she have imagined that her father was somehow part of it.

This new revelation, so casually delivered, floored her.

"I don't really know much of the details," he said. "The report is his Malaysian wife and kids were with him on vacation in Sri Lanka. He was in town when the tsunami hit and they were on the beach."

Suddenly everything changed drastically for Anna. Brock had opened up the world of her father to her in shocking bluntness. She didn't know quite how to deal with the idea of her father's *other* family, let alone that they were part of the quarter million tsunami victims.

"Is there anything else I should know about my father? Anything else that might shock me, or is that about it?"

"You'll have to make that decision when we get there." He finished his coffee. "Let's shoot."

Chapter 9

They drove the Humvee through a patch of jungle to a clearing about a mile from the main encampment. Anna continued to be very skeptical about being trained for possible combat in a few hours, let alone days, weeks or months. So what was really going on?

Besides, she didn't see herself as the soldier type running around shooting people and getting shot at. Nothing was further from her view of herself. If this guy thought he was going to make a killing machine out of her he was sadly mistaken.

It wasn't that she hated guns or anything like that. She'd done some target shooting with her mom's rifle and there were always guns in the house because of her mother's career as an outfitter, but Anna just wasn't keen on shooting animals for sport. If you needed to eat, that was different. But people? No way.

Before getting out, Brock explained the phases of training she was going to go through. First weapons, then stealth movement, hand signals and radio communication.

She listened intently, then said, "I'll do my best."

"That's all I can ask, Quick. Let's get to it."

"I have to warn you, I don't think I'm very good soldier material."

He nodded and stared off into the jungle for a moment, then he looked back at her. "I'm not going to make a soldier out of you. I'm just going to show you how to use a weapon. And then I'll show you some escape and evasion tactics. What you do with those tactics in the field will depend a lot more on who you were coming into this than on what I can teach you. Besides, no amount of training can make a soldier out of somebody who doesn't want to be one. I just don't want to die on that island because you didn't know how to stay with me in the jungle. Or because in a tight situation you didn't know how to shoot your weapon. I'm not doing this for you, Quick. I'm doing it for me. We clear?"

"We're clear."

"Good. Do me one big favor. Don't resist what I'm going to try to teach you. You save lives for a living. Well, there may be thousands of lives to save depending on how well you learn these lessons in the short time I have to teach you. So don't look at it like I'm trying to turn you into something ugly, like some pathological killing machine. I'm trying to turn you into someone who can save a whole bunch of lives. Okay?"

She could handle that point of view. It gave her a positive focus rather than a negative one.

"Okay."

"Thank you, Quick."

"You're welcome, Brock."

"Great. Now get out of that seat and let's do some work."

Brock introduced her to the operation of both the Heckler and Koch 9 mm MP-5K and the P-90. She handled both and decided again that she preferred the MP-5.

"Whatever you're most comfortable with is the best choice. Your weapon will be 4.4 pounds, thirteen inches, of personal defense. It carries either the 15-round magazine, or a 30-round mag."

Anna watched Brock. The man didn't handle the weapon, he caressed it. She could see that it was much more than just a tool for him.

"You can carry it in a briefcase, rucksack or against your belly. You live with it, it'll keep you alive. I shoot every day. We all do."

His eyes were bright with serious enthusiasm. There were no condescending scowls. She'd seen that plenty in her world of fighting fires—another male bastion that was slowly and painfully accepting the opposite sex into its elite ranks. But she knew he would push her hard.

"A team goes in light, but it needs to be able to put out serious firepower and this little baby will do it. And it's a whole lot lighter than a chainsaw."

"And deadlier," she added.

"Not in Texas," he came back, his expression deadpan.

Anna laughed. "No, not in Texas."

The man had a dry sense of humor under all that steely earnestness. She liked that.

"You've hunted and killed animals, right? Your mother being an outfitter."

"No. I've been on hunts, but I actually never hit anything."

"You've shot at animals?" Brock asked.

"Yes."

"You missed?"

"I did."

"On purpose?"

"Yes."

"Well, that's common. Most soldiers in combat over recorded history have failed to aim at their targets, or deliberately missed them. We'll deal with that. But you have seen death. You must have seen a deer shot, or something even more gruesome during a fire."

She flashed on a cabin she'd tried to save during a fire, where the two people living in it hadn't had time to get out. She never could get the vision of their charred bodies out of her head.

"Yes," she said, shuddering at the memory.

"Then you aren't a complete virgin."

However, she'd never actually seen an animal or a person take their last breath. "Can you be a partial virgin?"

"Absolutely. Sex and killing are very complex. The deed itself is almost an afterthought to the process that gets to the deed. I don't want to get philosophical about this, but becoming a gun-slut is as much a process as becoming any kind of slut."

Only a man like Brock would find a way to link sex and guns.

"You're very poetic."

"Yeah. The poet laureate of close combat."

Anna watched Brock disassemble and reassemble the rifle without once looking at it. He did this while talking the whole time. It was no more difficult to him than tying his shoes. He was good at his job. That was a comforting thought, considering the days ahead.

"It takes a long time to face the reality of killing. Society keeps us separated from the slaughter of our food, from the dying of our loved ones. I don't have the luxury of a slow introduction. I have to shock you into this world because where you're going, you might have to do what you're constitutionally and socially conditioned not to do. Kill another human being. Or more than one. And you have to do it automatically, with no forebrain interference. No thought. No judgment. And it *will* leave you traumatized."

He fired the weapon without warning and it shocked her back on her heels.

"That," he said from their crouched position, "is deadly force. It's not TV or the movies or video games.

They can work to desensitize you, but to use this for its intended purpose, you need to do just that. Use it."

He handed the gun to her. "Shoot that tree."

She started to stand.

"No. Don't aim, don't stand. Just point and shoot."

She followed his instructions. The gun had less kick than she'd expected, but the bullets came out so fast he had to grab it to stop her from emptying the magazine.

"Short bursts. That's all you want. Try it again."

This time she let go of the trigger after a couple of rounds.

"Good. Maybe you're going to be a quick study," he said with a smile. "Forgive the play on words. Your name just invites that. Follow me."

Anna smiled back. They walked down a narrow path where small mock buildings were tucked away in the jungle. He told her they were shooting houses, but she wouldn't need much practice there. He didn't anticipate any house calls on the island.

She began to feel a little as if she was being led somewhere that she didn't really want to go, to learn something she didn't want to learn, yet had no choice in the matter.

"I'm going to instruct your nervous system to a mode of behavior it's not used to," he told her. "I'm going to do it over and over and over ad nauseam. You'll get sick of me, sick of shooting. But you'll be better equipped in one day than you would be after several weeks of training. We have techniques that previous armies didn't have."

"I'm thrilled," she said.

He ignored her tone. "You have one great advantage over most civilians."

"Which is?"

"Your background."

"I'm a prime candidate to become an instinctive gun-slut."

"Yep. From now on, you will not rest. You will not eat. You will shoot."

They stopped at what looked like a rest station. There was a big table and bench, bottles of water and lots of ammo. Brock gave her a lesson on the parts of her gun, how to field-strip it, clean it properly and put it back together. Over and over and over.

After she went through the process about a dozen times he made her do it blindfolded. She couldn't. He straddled the bench, his knee against her thigh, his hands on her hands. He helped her find the parts, take them down and put them back together.

"What's wrong?" Brock asked after she shifted away from him.

"I'm trying."

She went to pull the blindfold away from her eyes, but he stopped her. "No. You're reacting to me."

"You're practically in my lap." She could feel his breath on her face.

"I'll be *in* your lap if you don't start focusing and forget you're female, I'm male and all the other crap that might flit through your brain. Damn, Quick, you'll be in the dark on that island night and day. You'll have night-vision goggles to see, but it won't help you if you have to break down a weapon because it got dumped in a mangrove swamp. Listen to me, you have to learn what I'm teaching you. If I strip you naked, I don't want you to lose focus. If I feed you worms covered in slimy crap, I don't want you to lose focus. It'll get us killed. You have to trust me. I am a fairly decent guy trying to save your life and mine, as well as your father's. Make up your mind. We're going into hell together, so we have to trust each other."

"You trust me?"

"I'm working on it."

"It's mutual."

He pulled her blindfold down. He was right in her face. She forced herself to remain calm.

Screw you, Brock. You want to stare me down it'll take you all night.

Two weeks of sleep deprivation and physical exhaustion had left her emotions raw. And her reactions. And her reaction to him was a mixture of anger and stubbornness—with a little flirting thrown into the mix.

"We're wasting time," she said. "Let's get this right."

She slipped the blindfold back over her eyes and took the gun apart and tried to put it back together. She did it with the blindfold off, on, off, on, off, and finally she got it right.

He made her do it right five more times just to make sure she had it.

"Good. Now we're making progress."

Next he showed her firing techniques from standing, moving, sitting and lying positions. She got used to him being all over her, correcting each movement. The term *hands-on* meant something to Brock. The guy was all about the business of training. A trait she had no choice but to admire.

The sheer violence of the submachine gun's fire-power astonished her. She expected not to be able to hit any of the silhouette targets that moved through the surrounding jungle. She didn't take long before she was beginning to hit some of them.

Brock wouldn't let her sight. She had to point and shoot, always looking at the target, never the barrel of the gun.

"You aren't a sniper. You won't be needing sniper techniques. You're going to be in jungle, forest, mangrove swamps and bamboo so thick you won't see three feet around you on all sides. It's damn difficult. Anything you shoot—snake, croc or man—will be very close."

She expected to dislike firing the thing, but by the end of a dozen clips she was bonding with the power of a damn gun even as she had a deep resistance to all that it stood for.

"Some people are naturals," Brock said. She studied his face to discover where she was in the crowd. She didn't always like it, but she was a bit of a sucker for praise at a job well done. He seemed to be complimenting her.

He said, "Just remember, a weapon is like a firefighter's pickax, you don't leave it lying around."

She corrected him as fast as he would have corrected her. "It's called a Pulaski."

"Listen up. A combat soldier's weapon is his, or her, Pulaski. Don't leave it anywhere. You take it to bed, the john, chow. Same thing, I imagine, if you're in a wildfire, it's blowing up all around you, you're running, you don't leave your Pulaski behind, do you?"

"If a fire is chasing me hard enough, I'd drop it and run like hell." She was half kidding, trying to lighten him up a little.

He stared at her quizzically, as though he was trying to decide if she was challenging him. He didn't seem to know what to make of her at times, so he just nodded. "Well, the kind of fire I'm talking about shoots bullets, so you might want to hang on to your weapon like it's your life."

"I will," she said.

"Then let's shoot."

Three hours later he started showing signs of being happy with her progress. She had to admit he was one of those teachers, or coaches, who figure their students out and feed them what they need. She liked calm and he gave her calm. She liked to know when she did something right and when she did something wrong without being screamed at or overpraised. He seemed to pick up on that. Or maybe he was just that way. She'd bet he'd make a great date.

They moved out.

Now the targets became hard to find. Up in trees, behind or in small stucco buildings that popped up here and there in the jungle.

She fired so much, the barrel of her gun grew hot and she had to switch with him periodically.

"Instinct shooting takes thousands and thousands of training hours to get down pat," Brock assured her. "You are only going to get thousands of rounds, so make them count. Will the bullets into the target."

Anna almost laughed at his last statement, but refocused quickly.

She fired left, right, overhead. She finally reached the point where she stopped thinking. Stopped trying to direct things, and just did as he asked her to do.

"That's it," he said. "That's what I want. The bird flies out of the brush, you swing and fire like a hunter with a shotgun."

Hour melted into hour. Her arms, hands and fingers were practically numb with firing.

Brock pushed her relentlessly through the course for six hours before he announced it was time to take a break.

"Quick, you've just fired more rounds than the average dedicated hunter will fire in a lifetime."

"It's been one of my goals," she teased, but he didn't catch the humor.

"Good. Before the night's over, you'll have fired more than the average squad of regular soldiers will fire in their entire tour of duty on and off the range."

She had several sarcastic comebacks, but decided it was inappropriate and even a little childish, so she didn't say anything. His enthusiasm for shooting hadn't quite reached her yet, but the necessity of it had. He'd managed to convince her that her abilities, what she was

learning, just might become essential to her and everyone else's survival. Including her father's.

Brock connected everything to the mission. He was
one of the best instructors she'd ever run into. Relentless? Yes. Obsessive? To be sure. But she knew herself
and she knew that, already, in a quarter of a day, she was
shooting the hell out of pop-ups and moving targets.
And she was doing it his way. Half the time she was hip-
shooting. Bird shooting.

If he can make a confident shooter out of me, she
thought, this guy knows what the hell he's doing.

Chapter 10

They munched PowerBars and drank from canteens during short break, breaks that were interrupted more than once by sudden movement in the trees and Brock's insistence that she drop and fire. She had no idea what was out there, but she did as she was told.

Then it was back to field stripping and cleaning weapons, blindfolded, in the jungle. He seemed to have endless patience. Definitely more than she had.

A thermos of coffee appeared along their trail, sitting on a small camping table, compliments of some unseen commando. A welcome respite for both Anna and Brock, although he didn't seem to appreciate it as much as she did.

After the short coffee break, Brock took both her

weapons, emptied them and looked them over closely. Then he reached into his backpack and came up with more ammo clips and reloaded them.

They talked quietly for a time as they drank their coffee while sitting next to the table. At one point, Brock went off into the woods and came back a few minutes later. "If you have to take a leak, you should do it now. We'll be going nonstop for awhile more."

Anna was hoping they were done, but his tone indicated they weren't even close. She did have to go. She got up and started to head deeper into the jungle.

"Hey."

Anna turned. He was glaring at her and it was the first time she'd seen something on the edge of real anger in his eyes. She stopped and looked around and there on the table lay her assault weapon. She went over and grabbed it.

"Shit," she said quietly, with a self-chastising grimace.

She didn't apologize, instead she went off into the woods with her gun slung across her chest, vowing to herself that it would never happen again.

When she returned to the table, she found Brock writing something in his small notebook. Probably keeping score of how many times she'd screwed up.

He didn't look up or say a word. She simply leaned up against a tree and waited for him.

That's when it happened. Dark figures appeared out of nowhere, guns blazing.

Her heart stopped.

Brock rolled and fired. She tried to do the same thing,

but couldn't get down fast enough. The blood paint sprayed all over her. She was now officially dead and her Glock had somehow fallen out of her hand and lay on the ground to her right as she had tried to roll away from the firing.

Then, just as they had magically appeared, the assailants were gone like phantoms. It had all happened so fast, so shockingly unexpected, she was dazed.

Brock, unmarked, took her weapon, pulled the magazine and cleared the chamber. "It's been in the dirt, clean it."

"You didn't have...real bullets."

She wanted to apologize, to promise she'd never make the same mistake, but Brock was busy with his global positioning system and the map he'd brought out of his pack. He simply wasn't the kind of guy who seemed the least bit interested in anything she might have to say. No excuses.

When she finished and her weapon was cleaned and hugging her body—he continued to ignore her—she tried to get his attention. "I'm ready. It's clean." She didn't like that her voice was a bit sheepish.

Without a word he was up and they were moving again. This time they were moving fast. He seemed to be in a huge hurry, moving low, silently, and controlling her with hand signals: stop, go, move left, right, circle back.

It was a long fast hustle through the jungle. Then he stopped and signaled her to settle in low behind the base of a tree.

They waited for a half hour, then another half hour

passed and they never moved. She could feel insects crawling up and down her arms and legs, the sting of mosquitoes on her neck, face and hands, but she dared not move or speak or even look anywhere but where he looked.

And then she heard something. Low voices. Men walking toward them. A chuckle. She saw them coming through the darkening green gloom of the jungle: four men in jungle fatigues. She had the feeling they were the assailants who'd ambushed them earlier.

Anna glanced at Brock. He had his weapon ready. She wanted to know what to do. Should she fire her Glock? What kind of bullets? Were they using blanks?

The men were coming right at them, oblivious.

Brock glanced over at her now and mouthed the words *fire up* and pointed over the heads of the approaching, unsuspecting soldiers.

Apparently she had real bullets this time, but she couldn't be sure.

She waited for Brock to make a move. And when he did, she joined him. They rose and fired up in the air.

Caught cold, the men looked chagrined at Brock and Anna as if they couldn't figure out how they'd gotten to this ambush site.

Brock smiled. "Nice night, guys. You heading into town?"

They grumbled and moved on. Anna secured her weapon in its holster on her thigh.

She was pretty sure this was something of a game with Brock more than it was part of the training. They walked a long way to get into position. He really loved this stuff. Creeping around in the jungle, hunting. He needed to get out more.

Later, as they were moving back down a trail, he said, "We covered about two miles of jungle to get ahead of them. Shocked them right out of their jocks."

Anna smiled to herself and put a star up on her inner blackboard. She'd screwed up earlier, but Brock looked pleased now. Stamina was the one thing she knew she had that could compete with these men. In her competitive, athletic mind she figured she could run more than a few of them right into the ground.

"You'd make a good sports coach," she said.

"My father was a coach. He was the Bobby Knight type. You know, the basketball—"

"Went from Indiana to Texas Tech."

"Right. That's the kind of coach my father was. I never liked that style. I'm more the low-key type."

She wanted to slam him with his own misguided vision of himself, but she let it ride.

"What did he coach?"

"High-school football." He smiled when he said it and she figured he must have reflected on some fond memories.

"You played?"

"Yep."

"You any good?"

"Pretty good. Quarterbacked to the state championship. Got beat by a field goal in the last ten seconds."

"That's rough. Any scholarships?"

"I had a few offers. I headed into the military instead. The military was something I'd been planning on for a long time. I think my father soured me on football. My grandfather was a soldier and I guess he was the one I really molded myself on."

Darkness dropped like a trapdoor, leaving them in the utter blackness. All conversation stopped between them. He had her apply a tiny bit of illumination tape to his back, and he did the same to her. He put another on the back of his right hand. Then he applied mosquito protection to her neck, ears and a dab on her cheeks. A little late in the game, but it helped.

Then he showed her how to use the night-vision equipment. "We're using a monocle so we can keep one eye adjusted to the actual dark. Just pretend you're looking out of it with both eyes, then look away with both eyes." She tried to focus on the trees ahead of her as he suggested. Everything took on a blurry green glow, and she could tell it was going to take some time getting used to.

Then he went a few feet from where they were and brought out some packs. He watched her as she strapped on her gear.

Satisfied, he turned and walked off the trail and into the jungle.

Just great. Is this going to go on all night? Maybe he wants to kill me here, so he doesn't have to take me with him on the mission.

No forest she'd ever been in was as black as this jungle. Except for the illumination tape and the night-vision goggles she wouldn't have been able to see anything.

Brock stopped alongside a small creek. Various jungle life slithered away. There was something that went into the creek that caused her to bring her weapon to bare. The jungle wasn't her first choice of nighttime jaunts.

Brock "cleared" a log with a penlight. "You don't want to sit on a booby trap." Then he said, "You didn't lay down fire on that first attack and you died. You did good during our ambush, so you're alive again. The thing I hate more than anything in this world is a funeral."

They entered a swamp. The cold water came up to her waist. They waded through this hell for another hour, then emerged into what looked like a rice paddy.

On and on and on until she thought she'd drop.

Did he ever get tired?

Suddenly they were right back where they had started. At the Humvee.

Brock made her put her arm out on the hood and he strapped some kind of complex thing to her wrist that resembled a digital blood pressure monitor but was much more complex. He turned it on and the band tightened. He noted the readings and pronounced that she would live to fight another day. He never explained what it was, and she was too tired to ask.

They got into the Humvee and sat in the darkness. He used a tiny penlight attached to the side of his helmet to write something in his notebook. She was curious as to what he was putting down but didn't want to ask.

Anna sat there in a near-comatose state of fatigue, listening to the sounds around her, and was amazed at the volume of activity out there. The predators and prey in their nocturnal survival dance.

Brock put away his notebook and flipped his night-vision monocular to the side of his helmet. He made a call on his cell phone, while Anna started to nod off. When he started to speak, she awoke with a start and tried to cover it with a cough. He didn't seem to notice.

"It looks like we're not leaving tonight. We'll resume training in the morning. How do you feel?"

She felt as if she'd been run over a couple million times and there was nothing left but a smattering of bones and sinew.

"My body lost that capacity a few miles ago."

"You have serious stamina."

"I know. But I think I might be at the bottom of the barrel."

"Our bodies are like cordless razors," he said. "It's best to nearly empty the batteries before recharging them. That's true of people as well. Intensity is the name of the game. That's what we train for. Endurance and intensity."

She stared at him for a moment, trying to get the analogy, but let it go, thinking it was a guy thing.

"Let's go home," he finally said.

Now, *that* she could understand.

On the way back to the base, Brock gave her an after-action evaluation. She was a fast study and had gone beyond his expectations. He attributed that to her being athletic, her firefighting skills, and even gave some kudos to her genetic heritage.

Praise was getting him everywhere at this stage. She laid her head back on the seat and smiled at the rather callow nature of her own thoughts. He was very attractive. She wondered if he handled his women as expertly in matters of the heart and bed as he did in matters of training. He was so disciplined, so rock solid, that when preparing for a mission he had total focus. Actually, she usually did as well. But she always liked banter. A little tension-releasing silliness. She wasn't seeing any of that in this camp. These guys all looked like serious Puritans heading for church.

She turned her mind to her father. What was he doing right now? Was he still even alive? Waiting? How badly was he hurt? Would she be able to get to him on time? Even though she was angry, she missed him.

Her early years in fire crews, then going into smoke jumping, had been eased by her father's reputation. Eased, but not with everybody. Women still had to fight for years to prove themselves. But she was privileged by walking in the footsteps of a firefighting superstar.

She glanced over at Brock and the reality hit her that she was going to jump into hell with this guy and she really didn't know who he was, other than some middle-weight soldier with a big résumé and the disposition and looks of Steve McQueen in *Bullet*. Divorced, no kids, living in a perpetual war, hunting and killing and rescuing and whatever else he did. That had to be a strange life.

At least firefighters had other careers, other interests outside of the burning season. Most of them anyway. She was, by her own admission, a bit obsessed. She'd never met a fire she didn't want to fight: Alaska, Canada, California, Washington, Oregon and Montana. Anywhere, everywhere. Dropping from the sky like some predatory bird to kill a small burn before it became a big one. Slog to a pickup zone. Drop in on another one.

She killed fires. He killed his country's enemies. She wondered just how different those two activities were. Until this day, she'd never thought of killing a human being. Never. It was just not the way her mind worked. But today she'd thought about it. Seen how it might happen. It was unnerving and fearful. She wasn't sure how she would react to the real thing. And how she would handle it afterward, if she survived. Would it change her? Make her into something she didn't want to be?

When they were almost at the camp, it began to hit her. The intense fatigue, the revelations about her father, the total depletion of her reserves. She began to nod off in the Humvee, and try as she might, she couldn't hold her head up.

All she wanted was to collapse.

"Quick, wake up. You're home."

She looked up as Brock pulled up in front of a small stucco building across from the Quonset huts.

"That's your quarters for the night. Try to get in under the mosquito netting or you'll wake up looking like a diseased raspberry."

She climbed out of the Humvee like a zombie. She

would have said good-night but didn't have the energy to actually form the words.

"Shit," Brock said to himself as he sat in the Humvee and watched Anna Quick walk away, her long legs scissoring the light of the lampposts next to the Quonset huts. He felt bad for her, all the burdens she now had on her shoulders. It amazed him that she could handle this after what she'd already been through.

It occurred to him, as a little aside in the back of his mind, that Anna Quick was one of the fastest studies he'd ever trained. He'd been looking at having to take her in with him as a liability, something to have to carry and protect. Maybe he'd lucked out.

Brock frowned with a bit of ironic smile attached. She'd gotten a little jumpy when he was up close and personal. Touchy. Well, she was a soldier for the next while and she'd have to get used to it. But he knew he'd have to be careful not to get too friendly. He was starting to like having her around—a little too much.

He had always been neutral on the arguments that allowed women into elite, tightly bonded, high-risk teams that engaged in hand-to-hand combat. Few men could make it into the teams. Fewer women would have the physical abilities necessary and many, like Swartzlander, argued that even if a woman did have the qualifications, even if she had the mental toughness, just adding a sexual component changed the dynamic. Men at the height of their testosterone aggressiveness, on a hunt-kill mission, working side by side with females?

Maybe there was something to that argument. Then again, maybe it was just a matter of adjustment. But case in point, all he had to look at was his own reaction. Already he was interested in this woman. How could he not be? She was exactly the kind of female he was naturally drawn to.

When they dropped onto that island with all that was there, would he be overprotective? Worried every step of the way about her? Would he become distracted from the mission?

These were very hard questions and he didn't have ready answers. But they were questions that would be answered in a very short time.

Anna had no idea just how bad this mission could potentially be. That little island was the scene of some bloody conflicts between government and guerrilla forces. It had been decimated by the tsunami. Entire coastline villages just vanished. Most of the population of the island gone. Now the loggers and interior farmers were back and burning the hell out of it. The fires were out of control.

And the guerrillas were hunting an American who'd fled there from his home near Kuala Lumpur.

Getting in, finding him, and getting out was going to be a real challenge.

Well, Brock thought, it looks as if I'm going to find out what a woman can do out there. But Anna Quick was different than any other woman he'd ever known. He hoped it wasn't a disaster.

Jason better have a damn good reason why he wants

his daughter there, Brock thought, feeling a sense of outrage and anger.

He watched Anna vanish into the building and found himself following her with his imagination, but he quickly cut that off and drove away.

Chapter 11

Tired, smelling of cordite, her brain swimming with all the training, and now weighed down with the gloom of knowing her father's grief and desperation, Anna felt heavy with sorrows.

She knew a lot of eyes were on her as she strolled back to the hut in the moonlight, her MP-5 slung across her chest, the Glock strapped to her thigh. For a brief moment, she'd almost forgotten that she was carrying firearms and not fire equipment, until she noticed a group of men watching her while standing near the mess hall. They were members of the strike team for Operation Fierce Snake.

The flower and the bees.

Or maybe it was the Venus-flytrap and the flies.

She imagined they were debating her ability, her presence. They probably thought it was utter madness to take an untrained civilian, let alone a female, on a mission like this. But they were wrong. And she would prove it.

When she walked inside her tiny barren room, she stripped to her underwear and T-shirt, dropping everything on the floor where she stood. She was way too exhausted for another shower, so she climbed in under the mosquito netting and collapsed on the hard cot. Just lying in a prone position was enough. She didn't need to be comfortable. Fire camps had trained her to adjust to almost every kind of bed.

She was just drifting off when she remembered Brock's admonishment about her weapons. She grabbed the Glock and tucked it in next to her on the cot. What would her fellow firefighters think of her now?

She lay awake for a few minutes listening to the hum of the fan. Everything was happening so fast she'd had little time to think, to understand and absorb what she was involved in.

To get herself to relax, she turned to more enjoyable thoughts. Brock.

Was he as good with a woman's body parts as he was with the parts of a rifle?

The thought gave her a momentary chuckle.

She sat up to check the mosquito netting for any openings, then lay back and fell asleep.

She slept hard for what seemed like a short time—until the world around her blew apart. Explosions went off on both sides of the building, flash-bangs of light and noise, blinding and deafening her.

Heart pounding, she sat up just as her door crashed open and bright lights blinded her for an instant. When her vision returned, automatic rifles were pointed right at her by men dressed entirely in black, their heads completely masked. They screamed at her in a foreign language.

Anna grabbed her weapon and rolled off the cot, ripping the delicate mosquito netting as she spun. Bullets slammed into the wall above her.

A man lunged for her as she tried to get her gun into play. He tried to jerk it free from her hands and the two of them crashed to the floor.

Other men, faces wrapped in black scarves, eyes like wolves, came in screaming and jabbing rifles at her.

She had to let go of her weapon. There was nothing she could to do to escape.

Suddenly her sleepy brain began to focus and she wondered how this could have happened. How could guerrilla fighters have taken over this camp?

One of the men, probably the leader of the raid, motioned for her to get up.

She did. Their flashlights blinded her again.

Helpless, trapped, not knowing if she was about to be killed, raped or taken away, Anna stared into the wavering lights and waited. The heart-pounding adrenal rush had abated. A tense calm came over her as she awaited the violence in whatever form it might come. Against the torrents of threats from outside forces, and the swelling tide of fear and desperation inside, she created mental barriers behind which she now retreated. She refused to let these men have victory over her.

One of her early instructors, a smoke jumper who'd been a jump master in the 101st Airborne, had said to her once that she had the kind of nervous system a person had to be born with. It wasn't something that could be trained into a person. Someone either had it or didn't. In a crisis, if your blood pressure spiked, you were wrong for dangerous work. If your blood pressure moved in the opposite direction, you were right. She thought of the test that Brock had given her earlier, and wondered if that was what he had been checking for.

A part of her wondered if this raid was actually real or just another test. She began to think it was a test. She dropped into stoic calmness.

One of the men grabbed her by the hair, forced her head back and put a knife to her throat. In broken English he screamed at her, "Who is your commander?"

"Napoleon," she whispered, defiantly.

"I will cut your throat right now. I ask you again, what is the name of your commander?"

"Napoleon Bonaparte and screw you."

"You want to die?"

She stared into his eyes, the only part of his face she could see, and thought of nothing, only the reflected light in his eyes and the retreating pupils and his harsh breath. She decided to take a chance that this was a test.

"Your breath stinks, Mohammad," she said. "You might want to try a good mouthwash before your next raid."

Another voice, speaking in a language she wasn't familiar with, said something and her would-be assassin backed off. From somewhere outside, she clearly heard somebody speaking English, and not as a second language.

Everything became still and quiet. She stared into the flashlights that were pointed at her and when nothing happened for a few seconds, she said, "This is all well and good, guys, but I'm really tired. If you men want to play war games, why don't you go find another playground."

Beyond the half circle of intruders she heard a soft laugh. Then, in clear English, "All right, everybody, get the hell out of here."

The flashlights turned off and the men with the guns retreated, leaving behind the stink of cordite. She was getting really tired of that smell now.

One man remained and he walked over to her, reached down and helped her up.

"That was a shitty thing to do," she said. "What I need is rest, not another damn test."

Tom Roca, his face now uncovered and visible in the faint glow of the outside lights from the corner of the building, nodded. "I needed to know how you would react under extreme duress."

"I thought that was Brock's job."

"He works for me. You passed with flying colors."

"That's because I didn't believe it for a minute. If a bunch of terrorists could get into this camp, with all that specially trained testosterone out there, then this nation is finished."

He stared at her as if he knew she'd made a valid point and he didn't know how to respond.

"Brock told me I was supposed to get some much-needed sleep."

"Brock doesn't run the world."

"Right now, he's running mine."

Roca seemed to have something to say, but he didn't get a chance to say it. Brock came in. "What the hell is going on here?"

"Just running some tests of my own."

Brock came back at him hard, angry and combative. "I have Quick on a training schedule. You don't inter-fere with that without coming to me first."

Roca got right in his face. "Don't come in here and tell me anything, Brock. Wait for me outside. Now!"

Brock never budged. "Get out of my face."

Anna watched the two men glare at one another like boxers in a ring getting last-minute instructions from the referee before the bell. Eager to go at it.

Anna didn't know what the protocol was around this camp, but it seemed to be a little out of whack. Military intelligence and CIA had communication problems and right now it was taking away what little sleep time she had left.

"Gentlemen, can I get a break here?"

Roca and Brock glanced at her as if they'd just re-membered what they were fighting about. Then they turned and walked outside.

She closed the door behind them, picked up her gun and crawled back under the torn netting and put her head down on the hard pillow.

Anna lay there for a long time thinking about the two men. They obviously had major issues and she was glad they weren't both going in with her. Not that she wasn't familiar with pissing contests in fire camps, but she expected things to be much different in the military.

So much for that illusion.

She closed her eyes, not caring what happened to her next, she wasn't opening them again until morning. To hell with the CIA, MI and Special Ops.

Exhaustion hammered her into oblivion.

The next morning, after she took a much-needed long shower and ran a comb through her hair, she got dressed and went over to the mess hall. When she walked in, nobody even looked at her. Men came and went as if she wasn't there. Things were getting worse, not better.

She noticed something else as well. The CIA guys were off by themselves on one side, the Special Ops guys were seated by themselves on the other side. Was it because of her?

One lousy female shows up and the whole place falls apart, she thought with sardonic bemusement.

Brock showed up, grabbed some coffee and eggs and sat next to her. He had a grim expression on his face. "You get any sleep at all?"

"The last couple of hours were deep and hard. I'll make it."

Brock glanced over at the CIA guys, then went back to his food. "Training under conditions of fatigue is the best way to learn things deep. Retention is much greater."

"Then I should come out of here an expert."

He smiled. She wanted to ask what was going on with the men, and maybe a few dozens other questions, but held back. She was just starting to get used to his rhythm and personality and wasn't ready yet to get too pushy. If he didn't like something, or had any problems, he'd get to them when he was ready.

They spent the day walking the range, firing hundreds of rounds, then repeating the course on escape-and-evasion techniques in the jungle. Brock was in a somber mood. He seemed preoccupied with something, and from time to time actually apologized for his distraction.

He went over the dangerous plants and animals that might be on the island, and told her about snakes and, no, there probably weren't orangutans on the island, though it wasn't all that far from Borneo.

Later that afternoon as they were going over the latest printouts from the satellite imagery and were discussing possible landing zones—the fires and winds were not making it easy and the location of her father was in the most inaccessible part of the island—Brock got a call on his cell.

He listened, said, "Yes, I understand," and hung up.

"We're going in at 2300 hours," Brock told her, folding the map and printouts and stuffing them in his pack. "Get some rest. It'll be all you get for the next few days."

As they were walking back to her hut, he pulled something out from one of his side pockets and then handed her a small bottle of pills. "You'll need these."

"Suicide tablets?"

He tossed her a thin smile. "No. *Go* pills. You might need to be awake for two or three days straight. Maybe more. They'll keep you alert and focused."

"Speed?"

"Provigil tabs. A synthetic form of natural brain chemicals that are produced in the hypothalamus—"

"I've heard of them. Lots of bad side effects. I don't like drugs and I'm used to staying awake for long stretches."

"Believe me, you'll need them. It's not enough to stay awake. You have to stay wide awake and hyperalert for days with no sleep. Your life, and mine, depends on that. No, they probably aren't good for you. Nothing in this business is. But I doubt that breathing smoke from fires is part of a healthy regime either."

She slipped the bottle of pills into her pocket. "I'll keep that in mind," she told him, and walked into her hut.

Chapter 12

She couldn't sleep. Not really. She was too tense and wired thinking about all that she had learned and worrying about her father, but when someone knocked on her door and she awoke with a start, grabbing for her weapon still slung across her chest, she realized that she had, in fact, slept.

She managed to pull herself up and went to the door. It was Brock telling her that it was time. She could see that men were already loading gear onto the jump plane parked on the small runway. Several choppers sat nearby. Amazingly, she hadn't heard anything come in.

"What's all that?" she asked Brock as they made their way across the road.

"The choppers are for the extraction team. They're

headed for the ship. The team will wait there until they hear from you."

"Me?" she said. "Wouldn't they be waiting to hear from you?"

He was about to answer, but got distracted by Verrill and Roca arguing about something, standing not more than fifteen feet away.

The men stood in the reflection of the runway lights, the sky above black and still, the moon tucked away in the clouds like a flashlight shining from the bottom of a dark pond.

Whatever was being said didn't seem to be sitting well with Brock. "Damn!" he grumbled.

He turned back to her. "Anna, go on and chow down. I need to deal with something."

"What's the problem?"

"A little change in mission plans. I'll be there in a minute."

Anna glanced at Verrill and Roca, then went on to the mess tent. The crew had apparently eaten and none of the other soldiers were inside.

She piled her plate high with cantaloupe, papaya, honeydew, cereal with berries, bread, meat loaf and more bread. A big carbo load for the jump.

When Brock came in, and she saw the look on his face, she knew something was wrong.

"How's the grub?" he mumbled.

"Fine," she answered, taking a bite of cantaloupe. It was a little green around the edges, but she didn't care. She was just thankful for the fresh fruit.

"Enjoy it. You'll soon be on energy bars for a while."

"What's going on?"

He didn't answer, instead he went for a cup of coffee and sat across from her, his face grim. He took in a deep breath and let it out slowly. "You're going to do great. You've learned a lot in the last twenty-four hours, Quick. More than I ever thought anybody could. Your reflexes are good, and your stamina is incredible."

Anna wasn't too sure where he was going with all the praise. "Just give it to me straight."

"I'm not going in with you. I've been pulled."

It took a moment for that to sink in. She put her fork down. "What do you mean you aren't going in with me? We've been training as a team for two days. I can't do this alone. I'll get killed out there."

"You won't be alone."

"Who's going in with me?"

"Roca."

She sat back in her chair, shocked and incredulous. Brock had a way of delivering news that always seemed to knock the wind right out of her.

"I don't understand."

"It's a CIA mission. They own it. All missions that are built on deniability are force-structured under control of the CIA or, in some cases, the ambassador. That's just how it is. Special operatives just do what they're told."

"But—"

"They can do what they want with it. I'm still involved, just not on the ground. I'll be on the ship. He'll take you in. I'll be responsible for the extraction."

"Is this part of the routine? Do they make these kinds of changes normally?"

"No. But there's not much that's normal about any of this."

"But he's not a soldier." Anna wasn't liking this one bit. How could Roca, a field agent, be expected to do what a Special Ops soldier could do? "So what happens if there's trouble?"

"He's been in nasty situations before. He's had a lot of cross training. He's one of a small number of CIA paramilitary. Where we have between forty and fifty thousand operators, the CIA has their own version. About a hundred and fifty of them. Roca is part of that team."

Anna remembered the shock attack when she was sleeping and how angry Brock was over that. "Did they ever intend for you to go in, or were you just responsible for my training?"

"I don't know. Apparently, I don't know anything."

"Can't you appeal to Verrill?"

He smiled at what seemed to be her naïveté.

Roca came in, glanced at her, ignored Brock, then went on to the chow table to get himself some food and coffee.

Roca put his tray down next to her, then he sat. "Anna, I need to brief you on a few things, in private."

She glanced at Brock. He got up and left. Roca went around and sat across from her in the chair Brock had just vacated.

Roca studied her intently for a second as if trying to

assess whether or not she was going to be trouble. "Sorry 'bout all the confusion. Can't tell you the reasons—" he gave her a look somewhere between sympathetic and smug "—but there are reasons. How's your food?"

"I'm not really all that hungry." She pushed her tray away.

"You're angry. I understand. Nobody likes to change horses in midstream. But this is a different world with a different set of rules and you just ride with the punches." Roca flashed a cool smile and his brilliant gray eyes. A greyhound among junkyard dogs.

She was still in a state of shock over this turn of events. None of the confidence she had in Brock easily transferred to Roca. Where Brock had calluses, scars and lines etched by extreme conditions, Roca was smooth and slick as an eel coming up silently from the bottom to grab you when you least expect it.

He sipped his coffee and rolled easily into a talking jag, telling her all about the activities of the terrorist organization Jemaah Islamiyah's agenda to create a radical Islamic state that would include Malaysia, Indonesia and parts of the southern Philippines, and how they had to be stopped now, before these sponsor states acquired nuclear weapons. He had a palpable obsessiveness about him that was a little unnerving.

"We're entering a critical phase against global terrorism," he said. "The jihadists understand that. They're going to hit us with everything they have, everywhere they can. They are becoming smarter all the time. The center of terrorism is moving around now, and it is here in Southeast Asia where it will be strongest if we don't nip it now. As Brock told you, your father had been running with the deepest agent we've ever had in their organization. That agent was killed, unfortunately. But not before your father secured a laptop that he believes contains vital information of an impending attack. One of the reasons I have to go in, at this late stage, is to see what that information is even before I bring it out. I have decoding programs I'll be taking along."

He ate a bite of meat loaf and sipped his coffee, then said, "I'm going to decode the data and uplink it by transmitter. Brock isn't as conversant—"

She had to stop him. She held up her hand interrupting him. "I thought Brock wrote computer programs for Special Operations training?"

Roca nodded. "He has, but that's not the same as what we're dealing with. Believe me, I'd just as soon not jump out of an airplane at thirty thousand feet onto a tiny island buried in smoke in the middle of the night, but that's what has to be done."

"You've never jumped from an airplane?"

"I've made plenty of jumps. Most of them static line hookups. Not much free-falling experience, I'm sorry to say. That's why we'll go in tandem. You get to control the jump so we don't lose each other in the fall."

Anna stared at her paramilitary CIA partner and hoped to hell he was half as good as Brock was.

"Brock will handle our extraction."

"I know. He told me." Anna didn't like the sound of any of this. "How many others will we have with us?"

"We're going in alone."

"What? A civilian and a CIA agent?"

"That's it."

"You've got to be kidding. You have combat experience at least?"

"Yes. I've been under fire many times."

She was going from partnering with what was probably the best cross-trained soldier in the military, to what? She'd probably do better if she were going in alone.

"You need to understand," Roca said, "that none of us, and that includes you, me and your father, are more important than the mission. Islamic theocratic totalitarianism is the last great challenge to us. This is the beginning of World War III. This is a systemic struggle and most of the Western world is just as asleep as they were in the 30's before Hitler woke them up. This time we're not waiting."

"I didn't think we were."

"Us, meaning America. But the rest of the world— France, Germany, Italy, Spain—they're still asleep. Still hoping appeasement will work. It won't. This is the last great war. We've beaten back feudalism and monarchism, fascism and communism. This is the final battle we'll face for a long, long time. America is in the position Rome was in at the beginning of the final Punic War with Carthage. Both Rome and Carthage were expanding. One was going to come out on top. It's the same now. The democracies are Rome. The dictatorships, whether fascist, communist or radical Islamist, are Carthage."

Anna didn't like getting world history thrown at her on the eve of jumping into a dangerous situation with a guy who was fixated on Carthage. She didn't know what to say.

Brock was just a soldier doing a job. Roca should, in her opinion, be talking about the mission and not politics. All his talk about entering the final war, World War III, was unpleasant enough, but in the context of having to go into perilous territory with this zealot and rescue her dad was enough to give her serious anxiety. Was he trying to impress her? Show her that, while Brock was just a mechanic, he was an idea man? A big-picture thinker?

I don't need a big-picture thinker, she thought angrily.

As if sensing her distress, he said, "Don't worry. I won't talk your head off during this operation. Just letting you know where I stand, and how important this is."

"Believe me, I'm perfectly aware of how important this is," she said.

Roca sat back and smiled as if he'd been successful at converting her. It would take a lot more than that to convert her to his cause.

He smiled quizzically. Then, apparently becoming aware of just how distant his audience had become, he changed the subject. "Anyway, your time at rookie camp was spent at Yakima Indian Reservation in Washington State, wasn't it?"

"Yes." She was sure he knew everything there was to know about her from the day she was born, and probably back to the day she was conceived.

"I hear the Indians really run you guys through the mill?"

She nodded, noting the politically incorrect reference. "They hauled us back in the Cascade Mountains to a tribal retreat, stuck us with a training crew and I spent every waking moment in the field digging lines, running portable gasoline-powered pumps and analyzing fire situations. They know their business."

"It's like a religion with them, isn't it?"

"Pretty much. It was hard, but it was fun at the same time. At night we'd compete in relay races. Then they'd set a corner of the reservation on fire and stick us out there with just minimum equipment."

"Nothing like live fire to bring it home to you. I hear the end of training is the great Northwest Indian salmon bake."

"Best salmon I ever ate in my entire life. My dad was a big salmon fisherman." She paused for a moment. "Do you know my father?"

She was surprised she hadn't thought to ask Roca before this.

"I've never met him."

Suddenly Roca was up and getting ready to leave. She took another couple of bites of her food, kept a hunk of bread and dumped the rest. They walked out of the building together but never said another word to each other.

Twenty minutes later, carrying all her gear, her MP-5 slung over her shoulder and her Glock strapped to her thigh, she headed for the plane. DeAngelo gave her a ride out to the runway. They chatted a bit, but she could tell he wasn't into it so they rode most of the way in silence.

When they got to the runway, the jump plane's engines were already warmed up and ready. She got out and spotted Brock talking to a couple of men. He gave her a little nod and a thumbs-up. She nodded and walked over to him. He broke away from the group.

"You stood me up on our first date," she teased, hoping she could get a smile out of him.

"You'll have to accept a stand-in. Sorry about that," he answered, but no smile.

"I hope he's as good as you are."

"He's not," Brock said sourly. "Just hope he's good enough."

"Thanks for the training."

"Trust your instincts and don't assume Roca always knows what he's doing."

She stifled a laugh. "Don't worry, that assumption isn't likely to occur."

"I see you've had a nice long one-way chat?"

"We have. Did you know, that during the Punic Wars…" She got a smile out of him.

"Once you find your dad, get him to any open ground, and we'll get you both out," Brock said. "Then you can tell me all about the Punic Wars."

"I think I'd prefer talking about scars."

He laughed this time. "You're okay, Quick. I'm sorry I'm not going in with you."

"Me, too."

They stood there for a moment. Then she said, "See you in a few days."

"Have a good jump. Give Big Ernie my best."

He knows about Big Ernie. She was impressed. "Will do," she said. She turned and walked toward the plane.

Brock watched her board. He laughed at himself for being such a kid. Damned if he didn't have a crush on Anna Quick.

DeAngelo strolled over. "What do you think, chief?"

"About what?"

"Getting pulled."

"Not much. Screw them."

"This is bad," DeAngelo said. "Roca's not up to this. No way. What about Quick, she handle this?"

"We'll see."

Brock couldn't find any way to support sending a civilian and a cocky agent into the situation by themselves. He knew sending a team was out of the question. Getting an entire team caught or trapped on a Malaysian island would be a political disaster. Indonesia and Malaysia were extremely sensitive about American troops. They even prevented most of the tsunami assistance from the military because of those perception sensitivities. But this?

"Let's go," Brock said. He had a bitter taste in his mouth and his anger was building by the second.

The rest of his team was already boarding the two MH-53 Pave Low helicopters for the trip to the converted freighter *Hammond* that was heading into the Strait of Malacca. A sea landing had been contemplated, but there were so many fast pirate boats and criminal gangs, along with terrorists, plying those inter-island waters that the idea had been scuttled.

Curtis Verrill was ahead of them, making his way to the choppers. Brock refused to get on the same bird. He doubted he could make the trip without getting seriously into Verrill's face.

Part Three
The Strait of Malacca

Chapter 13

Anna, nervously excited about seeing her father again, followed Roca up into the belly of the jump plane. This was the J-30, the updated version of the old workhorse C-130 that the forest service still used.

Roca introduced her to the two pilots. They showed her the digital avionics, moving map displays. She was impressed. "How fast can this thing go?"

"Fully loaded, we can clip along at over four hundred miles an hour," one of the pilots said. "It'll get us into airspace over the island in a little over four hours."

She followed Roca back into the belly of the plane

as its turbo-prop engines revved up to begin the taxi. Besides the two pilots there were only two crew members on board. A tandem parachute rig lay on one of the jump seats next to her.

Anna strapped herself in. She wasn't used to being in a plane without a team of jumpers and that only added to her tension.

Once they were airborne, Roca motioned for her to turn on her head mic. "How you doing, Quick?"

"I'm okay."

"Listen, should something happen to me, you need to know the code for the guide who's going to meet us. It's *Nero fiddles*. And the reply should be *While Rome burns*."

"Got it," she said, thinking Roca must have made this up. Half the people in the world would guess the second of that. It was all surreal. Anna hadn't really had much time to dwell on what she was doing. She was strapped in a seat on a plane actually headed for the island, memorizing a not-so-great code to give to some stranger who would take them to her dad. This picture, she thought, is a little out of focus.

She tried to go over everything that Brock had taught her, and hoped it was now so ingrained in her mind that her reactions would take over and she'd survive any ambush that might come her way. The thought of all that training somehow seemed to quiet her nerves, at least for the moment.

Brock had given her a roll of tape to cover any metal on her gear and to cover the muzzle of her weapon in the event they landed in water or a swamp. After they were airborne, Roca unbuckled and went up to the cockpit. She got the tape out and went to work on covering the muzzle of her gun and then looking for anything that might need covering or holding in place.

The packs they carried were watersealed, like the jumpsuits. Everything was fire resistant. When she went back to smoke jumping, she intended to lobby for more advanced equipment like this. Not only was this better stuff to jump with, it was so much lighter and had the ability to carry a cooling system, and a breathing apparatus. There were times when the onrush of modern technology bothered her, and times when she loved it. This was one of those times she loved it.

Anna went over a few more things Brock had taught her about escape-and-evasion tactics and handling firefights as she worked on making sure all her gear was well protected. When she finished with the tape, she decided to practice taking her MP-5 apart and putting it back together without looking at it. After a few tries she decided she had that down.

Then she checked her pack so she knew where everything was located in the event she had to get to something in the dark.

Anna still hadn't adjusted to the fact that she was going in with Roca, a man Brock didn't seem to have much confidence in. She thought maybe it was just something personal between them, but she had a bad feeling it was more than that.

Roca returned and sat back in his seat, strapping

himself in. "Your father's transponder is still sending signals, but we can't get him on the satellite phone. Hopefully there will be somebody to meet us at the lagoon on the east shore of the island. If there isn't, then we have to make it to a logging camp several miles in."

"Is there a village near the lagoon?"

"There was, but after the tsunami, some of those small islands never recovered. This was one of them."

Roca showed her prefire satellite photos and they discussed the winds and the best trajectory for the jump. The winds were their biggest problem. They were unpredictable. Sometimes they were there, sometimes not. She could only hope they didn't get much worse.

Four hours into the flight a green light blinked above the door leading to the cockpit. It was time to go.

Anna wondered if her father had changed much over the eight years. She hoped not too much. She loved his dry sense of humor, his quick wit. He was, like her, a ferocious competitor at everything he did. She figured some of her attraction to Brock had to do with their similarity in attitude. The two had worked together on operations in the past and she was sure her father had wanted Brock to come in with her. The change to Roca at the last minute was a little unsettling, and she wondered how her father would react to it.

One of the crew members helped them with the tandem chute. Having a tall man like Roca hooked tandem to the front of her was going to be uncomfortable and might block her vision as they were coming down trying to find a place to land.

Not a good start.

Oxygen masks on, the door opened, and they waited for the green light that would tell them they were on target. Adrenaline surged through her body as she waited. She took a deep breath and let it out to relax her anxiety.

The light came on and they stepped out into the night. Spread-eagle at thirty thousand feet, they quickly reaching 180 miles an hour as they dropped toward their invisible target below.

She glanced at her illuminated wrist altimeter and counted off the drop rate.

At six thousand feet the smoke loomed like a giant nuclear cloud. Beneath the smoke tongues of fire began to appear.

Anna always found free-falling exhilarating and great fun, but not this jump. It was nerve-racking and grew more so as the winds caught them. She felt as if she was skating a fine line between life and death with nothing to land on but fire or water. Burn or drown.

They crashed through the smoke columns toward the fierce reddish glow, the sensation like sliding down a coal chute into a furnace. She could feel Roca shaking against her body. The man was obviously scared. Just how many times had he actually jumped out of a plane?

She couldn't make out the lagoon and wasn't sure if the pilots and the spotters on the plane missed the correct drop zone. On her head mic she heard Roca swear. She agreed with every word.

"Roca, we're going to deploy now," she said.

"That's early, isn't it?"

"I need airspace. We might have to turn this into a glider."

She pulled the rip cord. The chute opened and they halted their free fall with a jolt.

She searched desperately for the lagoon. The fires must have exploded in the past few hours. The winds were fierce now. Were she by herself riding the winds, it would have been far easier, but with Roca's added weight, the drop rate was faster. More like a seagull carrying a fish bigger than itself.

She pulled the lines and glided with the wind to get more airspeed and longer air time. Neither of which helped them much. She desperately tried to outrun the flames below as she searched for the lagoon.

"We're going to have a hot landing. If we get hung up, cut and drop fast. Get the fire shield out," she said, forcing calm into her voice to keep him from panicking.

They broke through a swirl of smoke and there below them and rising fast were the fires of tiny Pouco Vulcao Island. She felt a strange, crazy awe at the sight of the raging furnace below. But there was no time to laugh. An updraft snapped up the chute and yanked them toward the flames.

Anna pulled hard on the lines, yelling, "Left, left, left!"

Spiraling surges of superheated updrafts spun them through the air like a wounded bird. The added burden of Roca made everything more difficult. Anna fought to keep control of the chute, to stop it from collapsing on itself.

They sliced in at an angle through the firestorm of

exploding embers swirling up from the trees. Glancing above, she saw that the chute was catching embers.

"Brace yourself. This is going to be a hard landing," she said. Roca didn't reply. He seemed paralyzed in front of her, a great slab of dead weight.

She saw it then, the black teardrop that had to be the lagoon.

They came in fast, dropping through the burning heat, their legs and feet skidding across the tops of flaring trees as tongues of fire hissed and snapped at them, the heat enveloping them with such intensity it was painful and difficult to breathe.

"Pull your legs up," she yelled.

He instantly obeyed her order and they tucked up their knees as best they could to avoid getting tangled in the burning treetops, from which there would be no escape.

They made it over the trees and sailed into the middle of the lagoon.

They hit the surface of the water, smashing into floating debris. Immediately they got tangled up in a mass of dead palm trees and the remains of several thatched houses that now clogged the lagoon. They sank beneath the black water.

The chute gathered around them like a burial shroud.

Anna struggled to get to her boot knife. The lack of oxygen in her lungs gave her precious little time. Never having trained for this kind of an emergency, and desperate to breathe, she fought off the panic. She broke open the harness to release the chute, but it was wound around them and tangled in rotting palm branches.

She worked quickly to cut herself free from Roca and from the debris.

Roca couldn't get untangled and he started flailing wildly and hitting her hard as she tried to untangle him.

You can't die on me now, damn you, Anna thought. He couldn't cut out before the mission was even started and leave her with nothing more than a code word and a map.

Anna reached up around his waist to find the snag. He nailed her pretty hard with his elbow and she had to fight him to get him loose.

She finally cut him free and raced to the surface, pulling him with her as she fought her way through the mass of rotting debris.

When they popped up out of the water, she took in a big gulp of much-needed air. Her lungs were burning from the strain. Roca gagged and coughed and belched out water. She held him with one arm and grabbed a tree branch with the other until he got himself together.

When she felt him regain control, she said, "You're okay. Just breathe normally. You're going to be fine."

Roca took hold of the tree and muttered, "Man…I thought that was it."

"You tried to take me with you," Anna said angrily. "Let's get out of here."

The south shore wasn't on fire so that's where they headed.

Their sealed packs had enough buoyancy to counter some of the drag as they pushed their way slowly through the rotting trees and thatch.

In the glow of the fire she thought it had a macabre

beauty, something Dante would have appreciated. Another circle of hell.

It took them what seemed like forever to dig their way to the shallows. The stink of rot, mixed with the harsh smoke from the fire, made breathing difficult and unpleasant. When she could finally stand, she stopped for a moment to relax her body and take in some deep breaths. Even the stinking air of the fire felt good, but her lungs hurt as if they'd just been ripped apart. She coughed and sputtered.

Something slithered up against her leg, sending a jolt of fear through her. "There's something alive in here. I felt it hit my leg."

"Just keep going." Roca said calmly. "Keep the knife ready. If a croc gets you, stab him fast. Go for his soft underbelly."

The notion of being eaten by prehistoric creatures in the firelight of a tropical lagoon kicked Anna into high gear. She suddenly had all the strength she needed to get out of there in a hurry.

They reached shore and sank into weeds like shipwreck victims, exhausted but happy to be alive.

Anna leaned back and rested her head on a wet log half buried in the mud and weeds. She lay there waiting for full recovery, astounded they'd made it over those trees and into the lagoon, and shocked by the world they were now in.

Roca made contact with Brock on the ship to let them know they were down and getting ready to move out.

Anna's moment of relaxation—tempered by the need

to find oxygen, and deal with the burning stink—didn't last very long. The wet log she had laid her head and shoulders on with an almost loving embrace…suddenly moved.

At first she thought it was some kind of mild earthquake. It took her a moment to realize that the wet log was actually *alive*. She jerked up. One word jumped into her mind: *python!*

The massive snake swung around incredibly fast, like a snapped cable. It got its coils around her before she had a chance to escape. It curled and curled and curled, its thick-muscled body the width of an elastic telephone pole, wrapping around her with a force unlike anything she'd ever experienced in her life.

The death grip took her breath away, the pressure unbearable…

Chapter 14

Roca tried to pull the snake off Anna but it was so massive and strong his efforts were futile. One of his arms was suddenly trapped between the massive curls of the snake's body.

Roca pulled out his gun and shot the snake in the head four or five times. It released his arm, but the body continued to coil and squeeze Anna.

The snake began to move, dragging Anna with it back into the water. She fought with every ounce of strength she had left, as Roca continued to shoot it. Suddenly the slithering monster released her and sank beneath the debris off the shore.

In shock, with her heart racing, Anna crawled back to the mud and weeds, trying for some composure. She stared at the water and debris for a moment. So much death and destruction. That one more body added to the mess would hardly have made a ripple.

"Southeast Asian pythons can get to twenty feet or more," Roca said, as if she needed to know that statistic. "Next time you lie on something, you might want to check it out first."

"I'll try to remember that," she grumbled as he helped her up.

"Let's clean our weapons and gear and get moving. Don't forget to take the tape off the muzzle," he ordered. He'd fallen back into his CIA-agent mode, giving orders, acting tough. But she knew the real Roca now. The guy gasping and fighting for air and shaking under her as they'd made their descent. She would never look at him quite the same way ever again.

They wiped down their equipment, broke down the weapons and cleaned them, and put them together again, then wiped out the inside of their helmets. But it was impossible to get the smelly mud off the outside of their jumpsuits.

Maybe, she thought, stinking like the environment would be an advantage in the same way hunters in Colorado spray themselves with elk urine to disguise their human smells. She stopped trying to clean off the mud, and just went with its added protection.

Roca pulled out his laminated map, GPS, and compass. They huddled together with a tiny penlight, trying to figure out exactly where they'd landed and how far it was from where they were supposed to meet the guide.

Apparently, they weren't at the right lagoon, so they'd have to meet the guide at the logging camp.

Anna was still shaken by the snake incident. "Besides monster pythons and crocodiles, is there any other man-eating creature on this island I should be aware of?"

"I don't think so," Roca explained. "But some of these islands have Estuarine crocs, they're saltwater, *Crocdilyus porosus,* and they're killers. Maybe the nastiest in the world. That couldn't have been what brushed up against your leg out there, or you'd be dead."

"Great! How big are they?"

"They can get to twenty feet long."

"What?"

"Yeah. Huge. They were getting near extinction, hunted for their skins," he told her, "but they're survivors. If you see one, don't think about it, just shoot the bastard. They're extremely fast and can be on you in a split second. Unlike the snake, if one of them gets you, you're dead. Right now, with everything running from fires, they're lying around waterholes like it's party time. So keep alert, and don't go lying on anything. If you have any inclination toward animal rights, shelve it."

Roca made a call to let the extraction team, now steaming up the Strait of Malacca, know their plans. He and Anna both wore transponders so the ship would always know their location.

They gathered up their gear and headed inland but had to leave the parachute partially visible in the middle of the lagoon. Neither wanted to go back for it. She hoped it wasn't discovered among the debris for a long time, that is, of course, assuming no one heard the gunshots at the snake.

Roca suddenly reached over and grabbed her neck. She started to jerk away from him, but he said, "Don't move," so she stopped.

He grabbed something off her neck and showed it to her. It was a large leech. Roca tossed it away. "Nasty little bloodsuckers."

She wondered what kind of diseases the little bugger had transmitted while it was sucking her blood.

"I thought these were great vacation islands," Anna said.

"Not these islands. They're not even on most maps. Been contested for years. Poachers, pirates, crime syndicates and Islamist terrorists rule them while Indonesia and Malaysia argue over their contending claims. We're at the northern tip of the Java Trench. It's a strange place." Roca then said, "By the way, Quick, I would have drowned. I appreciate what you did."

"The snake made us even," she said, amazed that he'd even admitted it.

Because of the darkness, Anna hadn't realized they were in the middle of a village until she nearly tripped over the foundation of a house. All around her were the marks of what once had been homes. It was like walking through a graveyard of an entire community. It was heartbreaking.

They made their way out of the village to the edge of a mangrove swamp. Their helmets had special earpieces and they could turn a tiny knob and amplify surrounding sounds. She turned the sound up and snapped her night-vision monocle down over her right eye. It was like looking into a shifting green sea. She was looking for soldiers, guerrilla fighters, but she was also looking for more snakes and giant crocs. She had a death grip on her MP-5. In a couple days, she'd gone from not being very fond of weapons, to embracing hers as if it was as important as her next breath.

Her mother had taught her to listen for sounds in the mountains that didn't belong there, her father had taught her how to survive in the middle of a firestorm and Brock had taught her how to shoot to kill. At the moment she was grateful for all three.

In the greenish gloom of the dense thickets, the root systems of the trees reached out of the swamp in tangled masses. Monkeys screamed and raced about in the limbs above. The stink of sulfides grew overwhelming.

In the peat bog, with its rotting, carbonized vegetable matter—the stuff that was the fuel that the farmers used to burn down the jungle for planting—Anna gazed anxiously at the crocs on a mud bank. They were huge, ugly beasts and they were bigger than canoes. They opened their giant mouths and made terrible hissing noises before slipping off into the water and disappearing. It gave her a shiver just to watch them, knowing there could be one around the next turn.

Then she heard a nasty snarl right behind her.

She whirled around. It stopped her heart. She pulled up her MP-5, but the croc slid into the water and vanished. It had moved lightning fast in the opposite direction. She let out a sigh of relief.

Fruit bats eyed her from vines hanging over the area where the croc had just been. I hate this place, Anna thought. We need to get out of here.

After an hour of moving around in the mangroves, they finally emerged into the high-canopied forest and dry land. It was her first moment of happiness since jumping out of that plane.

The canopy was so high and thick there was little growth on the ground. No sunlight could get through, which meant no ground cover. For a time they found the going easier on their legs, but the oppression of the air was unlike anything she'd ever felt. It was heavy and hot, and the mud-covered jumpsuit weighed on her. And the darkness made it almost intolerable.

Roca had made repeated attempts to contact her father, but got no response. She could only hope he was still alive.

Somewhere to their right Anna heard a muffled shout. Then in the light of the flames they saw movement: a half-dozen men, with rifles, moving toward the lagoon. She knew they'd find the parachute—and every guerrilla fighter on the island looking for her father would now be looking for her as well.

Bad thoughts began to pile up in her mind. Anna imagined herself and Roca found dead there on the jungle floor by some farmers. Shot down and left for the animals to feed on. She imagined no one even knowing how it had happened. CIA expunging all records of the operation. Her father dying. Her mother losing yet another person to the CIA.

Then she imagined herself alive but desperately

wounded and unable to reach her father. Her father captured, and tortured for what he'd done.

She knew she had to stop thinking grim thoughts like this. Brock had said something about the "go" pills being good not only for keeping her awake, but for keeping you focused. She didn't like taking anything beyond vitamins, but she decided this was the exception to the rule. Fearing she was becoming muddleheaded, she thought that the first chance she got, she would take one. She couldn't afford to be mentally tired and unfocused. That could get her killed.

They waited until the men were gone before moving on. Soon they came to a narrow river overhung with jungle. Now she had a glimpse of the volcanic mountain ahead of them, visible in the glow of the spreading fires.

That's where they were headed.

Roca stopped. She came up alongside him. He was staring off into the jungle. He pointed and she stared but saw nothing. He made a gesture as if to say he thought something was out there but didn't know for sure.

After a minute, Roca motioned and they moved on. It was much like following Brock through the jungle in Guam, except for one big difference: She didn't expect to be killed there.

Every step, every second she was on this island, she anticipated an ambush.

Suddenly she realized they weren't alone. Something, or somebody, was moving in the same direction about twenty or thirty yards away from them. Her hearing device picked up what her eyes could not.

"Roca, I think we have company," she whispered.

They stopped, so did the source of their concern.

"You see anything?" Roca whispered back.

"No. But I'm sure there's somebody, or something, out there."

Both of them trained their weapons on the jungle.

"There." She saw a person—or was it a monkey—moving between tree trunks in the green gloom.

"Yeah, I see it," Roca affirmed. "Let's get out of here."

Anna followed Roca into a tunnel of blackness, ducking branches, the smoke pungent in her nostrils. They were practically running now.

All communications now came from hand signals.

The farther they went, the more active the jungle became. Every living creature seemed to be on the move and it was unnerving not knowing what was out there.

And if it was human, why hadn't that person attacked?

The Hammond

Brock turned to DeAngelo as they stood in front of a bank of monitors. "Where are they now?"

"Not very far in. At the rate they're moving it could take another hour or so."

"What's holding them up?"

"They got that bad start after the jump into the lagoon where Anna met the python. Now its one of those one-thing-after-another deals. Roca is keeping us updated."

Verrill paced behind them like some nervous, expectant father. He kept complaining, asking when the new satellite pictures were coming in.

Brock was still so furious about being pulled, he hadn't even spoken to the CIA officer since leaving Guam. He turned now and said, "We need to send in that expensive little drone we're sitting on. You won't get any better pictures from space."

Verrill looked at him, but didn't acknowledge the suggestion.

It had made no sense to send in somebody like Roca. He wasn't experienced in jungle warfare.

Verrill didn't seem to believe an explanation was really necessary. No matter how much education or training a Special Ops soldier might have, according to Verrill, they were just grunts, blue-collar boys.

Brock knew that some of his anger was because Roca was there with Anna. He had to acknowledge that he'd made a connection there and he hated that he wasn't on that island with her. Maybe he'd gotten too preoccupied with her and wasn't seeing straight. Perhaps Swartzlander was right about mixing women and men at this level.

Brock knew he had to calm down and focus on what was ahead of him. It wasn't his mission anymore. It was Roca's, and it was Brock's duty to follow orders and go along with whatever the CIA had planned. He was there to assist in any way they wanted.

But he couldn't shake the fact that this was the first time he'd been pulled off a mission. And the first time he'd been involved in an operation run like this. He wondered if Special Operations Command, SOCOM, was directly involved. Were the commanders at MacDill Air Force Base in Tampa monitoring the operation via their Blue Force Tracker communications system? Just how sensitive was this? He had a dozen unanswered questions.

He went up on deck to cool off.

They were moving steadily up the Strait of Malacca at eighteen knots. Just another cargo vessel. If any hijackers were to make an attempt at taking over the ship, they'd be in for a big surprise. Beneath the false exterior lay enough firepower to take on anything.

The two Pave Low choppers were hidden beneath giant tarps freighters used to cover on-deck cargo. The ship had torpedo tubes that SEALs used to move out into the sea. There was every kind of sensor and navigation instrument a fighting ship would need. And they had satellite connections to the world. The place was a floating palace of high-tech. Brock had been on four missions in the past with this ship and she was a beauty under an ugly exterior.

Swartzlander joined him up on deck. "They still haven't reached the target."

"I know," Brock answered.

"Something stinks about this," Swartzlander said. "We're out of the loop completely."

Brock stared across the dark sea, listening to the soft chop against the hull. The lights on an oil tanker they would pass in an hour or so twinkled in the distance. Dawn was going to break in a couple of hours. That's when Anna and Roca would become most vulnerable. He stared at the plumes of smoke in the distance.

Two chopper pilots, Reiter and Frye, came up from under the chopper tent with a seaman.

"Everything ready?" Brock asked.

"When you tell us to fly, we fly," Reiter said.

"Soon as we get our man in place, we're going," Brock assured them. He turned back to the sea.

Brock had worked hard to rid himself of his early reputation as something of a rebel. He didn't want that suppressed part of his character to resurface, but this was just the kind of top-heavy operation that could set him off.

His team was used to great respect. They were not used to being left in the dark, treated like minor actors on the CIA's stage.

He couldn't be sure if this was an operation cooked up by the new intelligence czar, the director of National Intelligence, or something Verrill was running on behalf of the ambassador to Malaysia.

Being attached to a task-organized secret assignment where source information was kept to a very minimal need-to-know, and where the possibility of internal disinformation was very high, had Brock in a box.

"We need to get a drone in there to look around."

Swartzlander nodded. "We're getting it ready now."

He had no levers to push, no avenues to travel. He was stuck. What made his case worse was none of his people were on that island. The CIA had turned Brock's team into a damn taxi service hired to pick up whatever was coming out...if anyone was coming out.

Chapter 15

Pouco Vulcao Island

A smoke-jumping friend of hers had called it "Anna's extra gear."

When it seemed she could not possibly have anything left, when her reserves were depleted and the muscles had been pushed to their max, she'd get this incredible second wind: an extra gear.

Almost miraculously the fatigue had lifted, her mind was clear and she was ready for another big push. She didn't need the "go" pills. Her "go" was inbuilt.

As they moved along a reeded mudflat on the edge of the forest, Anna saw the shadowy phantom that was tracking them again. Much farther away this time. The figure was no monkey or orangutan. It was definitely a person. Someone who didn't have the advantage of night-vision and couldn't know Anna was tracking him.

Then the person vanished.

Anna hoped it was a native and not the scout for some guerrilla patrol.

They weren't as close to the logging camp as Roca seemed to think. She'd been tracking their progress with a topo map and while Roca could read it, he didn't seem to understand just how slow they were going.

Her confidence in Roca was still on hold. He denied her input on several occasions, but then relented. He had an uncertainty about his moves, the way he had to stop and look at his directions constantly, then communicate back to the ship. All of it struck her as worrisome.

She wanted to take over and show him how to find and integrate visual markers and changes in terrain. Reading maps was only half the game. But when she tried to show him a few tricks, he got a little angry. "I can handle it, thank you."

"I've been doing this all my life, both as a mountain climber and as a firefighter. I know how to read beneath the surface where the terrain dictates."

That seemed to trigger an element of hostility in Roca she hadn't seen before. But Anna wasn't interested in placating his sensitive ego. Not with her life and that of her father's on the line. "Look, it's not enough to be able to use a GPS receiver with a map overlaid with a grid of coordinates. It only tells you so much, and that's if you can even trust the GPS with all the atmospheric interference."

Roca backed off. "Go ahead, then. Lead the way."

She replotted the course and decided they were moving off-line and were at least another hour from the logging camp at the pace they were going.

Roca nodded with a frown when she explained it to him. She didn't know how much experience this paramilitary CIA guy had with calculating trekking distance and time, but she figured not that much. Undoubtedly, somebody with him handled that chore. If, that is, he ever did any hard trekking.

Without any further discussion, Anna took the lead. Finally she felt more relaxed. Even if she couldn't trust Roca, she could trust herself. They pushed on, with the fires raging only a few hundred yards away. They ducked through tangled vines and leaves, climbing roots and slogging across murky rivulets.

She spotted a giant croc. It was about fifteen yards away, on the bank of the stream, its mouth wide open and pointed in their direction. She had never wanted to shoot an animal before, but on this occasion she was happy to have her gun handy, just in case.

There were other creatures moving around. Vines that looked like snakes, snakes that looked like creeper vines. And there were quick-darting creatures that made her start to swing the gun before she realized that whatever it was, meant no harm to her.

The air wasn't as smoky deep under the canopy, but

it was painful because they were moving fast, breathing heavily, taking the smoke deep into their lungs.

The first hint of daylight seeped in through the top of the canopy, making the trees seem luminous. As they were coming up to what looked like a road, they spotted guerrilla fighters coming down the road. Three of them. They wore face scarves and carried their weapons pointed in front of them. They were moving fast.

Her stomach tightened. They stood frozen about thirty feet from the road and just watched the men pass.

She and Roca waited for about ten more minutes in case there were more men, then they crossed the road and headed back into the jungle.

Snakes and crocs took a back seat now to men with guns. Whatever visions she'd had of what soldiers faced, it was nothing like the reality. She was sure the deserts of Arabia were bad news, and the treacherous mountains of Afghanistan, but now she began to sympathize with Vietnam vets and all who had ever fought in a damn jungle.

The random violence of normal life, accidents, crazies, even firefighting, was one thing. Being in a world where there were armed humans who wanted nothing more than to kill you, animals that wanted to poison or eat you, that was something else.

It wasn't just fear so much as it was the elimination of all awareness but the moment. No idle thoughts. Just the absolute moment, looking, listening, preparing to face purposeful, directed, deadly force against her and Roca. There is a constant, relentless tension. Even in a fire she could get to safe ground and take a break, rest, eat without looking over her shoulder. Not here. Resting and eating were the most dangerous times.

They were moving along at a nice steady pace when they stopped abruptly. Through the trees, not more than thirty feet in front of them was a small encampment. Two men were squatting, holding bowls, eating what appeared to be rice. A third man, his rifle slung over his back, was folding what looked like a hammock.

She and Roca hadn't been spotted, so her instinct was to retreat, go back some distance and circle around the camp.

Anna started backing away, slowly, but Roca went forward—and started shooting.

She stood back, motionless.

The three men in the camp never had a chance. Roca killed each one before they could get to their guns. Then he walked into the camp to check the bodies. She reluctantly followed, but couldn't absorb what had just happened. The sudden violence, the bodies lying on the ground in death throes where, moments before, they'd been quietly having a morning meal, breaking down their camp. She was stunned.

One of them was still alive and she was about to take off her pack and get her med-kit, out when Roca walked up and shot the man through the ear. She jumped back, startled.

Roca turned to her. "Let's go." He said it as casually as if they were simply out for a morning walk and she was lagging behind.

Ann was too shocked to say anything.

This time Roca took the lead back. She was in no shape to be leading anybody.

Anna hung back, replaying the scene over and over. She was extremely agitated and conflicted by the entire gruesome scene. Killing those men had seemed unnecessary. Plus, it would tell their enemies what direction she and Roca had been moving since leaving the lagoon. But there was a lot more churning around in her mind. Had there been some military necessity to killing those men she didn't understand? Why else would Roca have reacted so violently? Anna searched for a reason but couldn't come up with one.

After a while, she wondered if she would have been able to shoot if the situation had been turned on its head, and the men had come after her.

She'd just started to get more comfortable with Roca, but this incident threw her. The only justification she could see was that he'd assumed they couldn't possibly back out of there without being heard. And that would then have given the men the opportunity to get their weapons and come after them.

Please let that be the reason.

On the other hand, Roca had killed them without hesitation and with such cold-blooded ease that it boggled her mind. No matter how much she'd seen this on TV, or listened to Brock try to describe it, the reality was very different. Nothing, not car accidents she'd witnessed, not people burned in fires, nothing was quite like watching a man shoot three men dead in the way she'd just witnessed. It was chilling, and gut-wrenching. She felt nauseous.

But now she understood clearly what Brock had been trying to teach her. To kill like that was not the normal mind-set. One had to be either crazy, or very well trained and conditioned. It didn't matter whether it took place in some street gang or in the military. Either way, Anna didn't think she was ready for it.

Doubts that she thought she'd beaten, that she'd hoped Brock had somehow excised, were back and they were back with a vengeance. She wasn't sure, having seen it in all its horror, that she could do it. Just blow somebody's life away. She feared she might hesitate and that hesitation might get herself or somebody else killed.

The suddenness and violence of war was much like a wildfire that could lay calm in one minute, and explode in her face another.

But that was the only real comparison. Firefighters might give fire living characterizations, call it a monster, fickle, a dragon, but it wasn't this. Nothing had prepared her for killing people, or being killed by them. All the horror movies she'd ever seen wrapped into one couldn't come close to the feeling she had now. It wasn't fear in any way she'd known it before.

Maybe it was that she believed she could always outwit fire. That she was aware of all the variables it brought and she knew how to deal with them. Study the mistakes of others was the mantra of one of her bosses in the early days when she was a ground pounder.

Combat was a whole new world to her and she didn't like it and didn't feel as if she understood the rules, or knew the variables. Brock had taught her all he could in a day, but she sensed it wasn't nearly enough.

She followed Roca in a mind fog, until he suddenly stopped and she realized they were lost.

"Goddamn," Roca said as he tried to find an opening where they could see the volcano, their main marker.

"Who were they?" Anna asked quietly.

He turned to her. "What?"

"The men in that camp. Do you think they were—"

"Hey, we don't have time for after-action analysis. They were the bad guys and we're the good guys. Those men were in our way. I don't care if they were poachers, pirates or jihadists. No more discussion. You're the great woodsman. Get us back on track. You don't have time to fret over the past. The *Hammond* will be entering its designated pickup location in short order, and we have to hit that window…with your father. And right now every damn guerrilla fighter on this island is our enemy."

For now, she would have to let it go and focus her attention on getting them to her father. She checked out the map and proceeded to get them back on course to the logging camp. This time, she wouldn't let him sway her from her objective. She knew exactly which way to go, and she knew exactly what she had to do when she got there.

"It's not much farther. Less than a quarter mile," she assured him.

He nodded and followed close behind.

They had been walking for about ten minutes, when Anna looked up from her thoughts and found herself staring into the wide eyes of a young girl standing not ten feet away, like an apparition that just materialized out of thin air. Had it been an enemy soldier, she'd be dead.

The girl looked to be about nine or ten years old. She had jet-black hair cut short, coming just below her ears. Her blue eyes were stunning, peering out of such a dark little face. She wore simple cotton pants and a dirty green shirt. She was barefoot.

"Hello," Anna said. "What are you doing—"

Roca spun around. Anna grabbed his arm. "Don't shoot! It's just a child."

But the sudden movement frightened the girl and she ran off and quickly vanished.

The idea that some little girl had been nearby when the shooting took place scared Anna. The child might have been hit!

"She might be working for our enemies," Roca protested.

"You can't shoot a child."

"Kids, in this part of the world, can be as deadly as the bombs they carry, or the information they deliver. Anna, this isn't a resort. Nobody here is your friend. Everybody here wants to kill you."

"I can't believe that child wanted to harm us. What if she's just hungry? Or she's hurt?"

"We're here to get your father off this island. We're not the Red Cross. Nothing else matters. Now let's go."

They started moving again. Anna was obsessed now with the little girl, finding her, communicating with her and keeping Roca from shooting her.

Was she the one following them?

The winds rolling over the island changed and they had to put on smoke masks. The heat came with the change and Anna felt as if her skin was going to peel off. She sipped from her water bottle at every stop to keep fluids in her body and wondered about that little girl. The child had no smoke mask, no water bottle, not even a pair of shoes on her feet. How could she survive?

They refilled the camelback water bottles in a stream, dropped in pellets to kill everything that might hurt them, then moved on.

They were climbing now and more sunlight filtered through the trees in thin beams. The ground cover grew heavier as the canopy grew less thick above.

Anna saw the girl again.

This time she grabbed Roca. "Don't move. Don't do anything. Let me handle this."

Anna motioned the girl to come closer. Instead, the girl held her finger to her lips, telling them to be quiet. She didn't move and neither did they.

A few minutes later they heard men talking. The voices approached, then began to fade.

The girl continued to caution them to be quiet for another minute. They heard somebody moving in the same direction of the other men.

They waited. Finally the little girl walked over to Anna. She stopped and said, "While Rome burns." She seemed very proud of herself at first.

Anna glanced at Roca. Then she turned back to the little girl. "Who sent you?"

"Oh, wait, I didn't do it right," she said in perfect English. "You were supposed to say something first. I messed up."

"You did just fine," Anna said, smiling.

"But you have to say something first before I said, 'While Rome burns.'"

"Nero fiddles," Anna came back.

The girl smiled. "Okay. I'm sorry."

"No problem," Anna said.

Roca said, "You are the guide Jason Quick sent?"

"Yes." She stared at Anna for a moment. "You're Anna?"

"Yes."

The girl came over and stuck out her hand. "I'm Azalina."

"Very nice to meet you, Azalina." Anna shook her hand. "This is Tom Roca."

Azalina gave Roca a darting glance, but made no effort to go near him.

"You're going to take us to Jason Quick?" Roca asked, sarcasm staining his voice.

"Yes," Azalina answered, all proud of herself.

"Christ!" Roca shook his head.

"How is he?" Anna asked as gently as she could. She could tell the girl was a little scared of Roca.

"He's sick. His leg is all bandaged up. And he sleeps a lot, but he'll be better now that you're here."

Anna removed her helmet with all its Space Age-looking gear. She didn't want Azalina any more frightened than she already was.

Azalina said, "We have to hurry. Many bad people are here in the trees. They will kill us. Follow me, I'll take you to him. We have to go up the mountain."

Anna took an energy bar from her pack and handed it to Azalina. "You must be hungry."

Azalina's eyes lit on the bar like a mouse on a piece of cheese. She accepted the bar and ripped open the package, broke it in two and put half in her pocket and wolfed down the other half.

"You're very pretty," Azalina told Anna.

Anna smiled. "Thank you. And so are you."

"Girls, let's get moving," Roca said impatiently.

Azalina danced ahead of them like a puppet, disappearing and reappearing, motioning them forward, pointing to an invisible trail. They climbed through copses of thick bamboo, then high grasses, then dense foliage.

After about an hour of this they reached the edge of a narrow river where Azalina showed them where she had a dugout canoe hidden.

Roca grabbed one side, Anna the other and they pulled the canoe into the water.

They climbed in with Azalina in front, Anna in the middle and Roca on the other end.

"How far?" Anna asked.

"Not far," Azalina answered. "We have to go down the water past the cliffs. It's the best way. The soldiers never come this way. They use the road and logging trails."

"How far up the mountain is Jason?" Roca asked.

"He's up in a secret cave. They'll never find him. Only people who lived on this island know about the caves. Most of those people are dead or have moved away."

The matter-of-fact tone and the way she looked straight into Anna's eyes without any sign of intimidation made Anna fall in love with Azalina instantly. When she stared at Anna for a moment and smiled, it sealed the bond that was forming between them.

Azalina took a pole that was twice her size and used it to push the canoe along the narrow waterway.

Jason Quick believed, in moments of clarity, that he was now dying. They wouldn't get to him in time.

He wondered if Azalina had found them, or if she'd been taken by the men looking for him. They would make her talk, force her to give him up. He never should have sent her. She was too young. Too innocent.

Jason didn't know what was causing the severe delirium. He'd had inoculations against so many Southeast Asian diseases that he couldn't remember them all. But something bad had him in its grip.

He thought of his boys and tears came to his eyes. Jasni and Majid. Gone. Seri, his beautiful wife, gone.

In his desperate wariness and his pain and delirium, Jason knew only that he must hold on. Azalina would find Anna. Azalina, so strong and too smart for her age.

The Jemaah Islamiyah soldiers wouldn't get her. There had to be limits to the horrors of one's life. The universe just couldn't be that blind, that disinterested.

Chapter 16

Anna thought her father had very likely been saved by this young island girl and her family. That perhaps Azalina lived in a village up in the mountains and had been sent by her parents to find Anna and Roca and lead them back. At least that was the scenario Anna contemplated as they made their way to her father.

When they reached the base of a lava outcrop, Azalina pointed. "That way is the best. We'll go up the mountain. There's a bridge we'll go over to the other side. It's the shortest way."

"What kind of bridge?" Anna asked her.

"Just a little one. Made from ropes and bamboo. It's strong enough to hold all of us at one time. I know because I've seen whole families cross it."

After hiding the canoe, Roca took out his Sat phone and walked a few feet away to contact the ship. Anna was more interested in getting more information about her father out of Azalina.

"You said Jason has his leg bandaged. Can you tell me more about that?"

"It's on his leg—" she pointed to her left leg at the thigh "—about right here. The bullet went right through. I saw it. He has two holes. One on the front and one on the back. I think it really hurts because he doesn't like for me to touch it."

"Can he walk?"

"I guess so. He climbed up to the cave. But he's worse now. He doesn't have any more medicine and there's only a little bit of food left. I stole a soldier's pack and it had some food and a flashlight, but only a little medicine. He has a fever. He sweats all the time and… shivers, and sometimes he talks funny and I can't understand him."

Her dad must be in pretty bad shape. She was anxious to get to him.

Roca finished talking and walked back over to them. "The ship is about six hours from coming into position for an extraction. We need to get moving."

Anna had a ton of questions to ask Azalina. She wanted to know everything about her and her family. Had they all survived the tsunami? Had they gotten the aid they needed? And how long had they known Jason? But the questions would have to wait.

Azalina led them into another thicket of bamboo and

they had to hold on to each other as they pushed through.

Anna had always considered herself savvy in the mountains and had spent endless hours and days climbing and trekking, often alone, but Azalina was way beyond anything she'd even imagined herself doing, especially at such a young age. This was an extraordinary little girl.

Azalina moved up the mountain with ease. She would turn every so often to make sure they were right behind her.

At one point they could see out over the island. Four massive smoke columns rose hundreds of feet into the air. The winds had died down to almost nothing. A still had come over the jungle island.

The climb steepened. The thick tangle of fronds and vines gave way eventually to the rising slopes, and steep rock cliffs, like great barriers. Anna couldn't see anything that even resembled a trail, but apparently Azalina could.

Anna remembered when she was Azalina's age, hiking in the mountains of Colorado with her parents. They were some of the greatest times of her childhood. Her dad would stop constantly to point out a particular plant or tree or an animal that had great climbing abilities like the mountain goat or the tiny pika.

They'd spotted a pika one day on a climb. A soft little ball of light brown fur, no bigger than a hamster. The round-eared creature didn't even have a tail, and made a strange noise, sort of an *eenaanck* sound that had made Anna laugh. Azalina somehow reminded Anna of a pika, she was just as agile and just as tiny, but had no fear of the mountains.

She remembered all the hikes she and her dad had taken together and how he liked to tell her about the Colorado mountains and the great things that had happened there, and occasionally the bad things, like trophy hunting. Both her parents didn't believe in it, and her mother would never take out a group of trophy hunters, no matter how much they offered her. She only took photographers, nature lovers and meat hunters during the seasons, but never trophy hunters.

Her parents had despised the trophy-hunting mentality, the search for records. They thought it was a disgrace to the whole history of hunting for food. Her dad could talk for hours on the subject. What kind of man was he now? she wondered. She'd always thought him the best of fathers, the best of men. But he'd left her and he had another life, a secret life apart from her, and it was something he'd wanted more than her and she had trouble with it. He'd brought her great pain, great sorrow.

Concentrate, Anna told herself as she tripped over a rock but then caught herself. She had to narrow her mind to the present emergency and not drift back to the past. She knew that. She lived that way in the fire jumps, but her father had triggered so much emotion. So many memories.

Anna was worried sick now about her father's condition. When Azalina was describing the wound, and the apparent delirium, she had a frightened, constricted look on her face that told Anna more than the words did. The child had, no doubt, seen far too much death and she knew what she was seeing.

When they stopped to rest, Anna asked Azalina how long ago it was since she'd seen Jason.

"Yesterday. Before dark," Azalina answered.

"Does he have food? Enough water?"

"Yes. There is a waterfall and pool not very far from the cave. He has plenty of water. And fruit. I like to bring him fruit."

"But where do you live?" Anna was digging for information.

"I live there."

"In the cave?"

Chapter 17

It had been difficult getting Roca to open up. But now, all of a sudden, he was joking with Azalina. The girl didn't explain about living in the cave, and Anna didn't want to push it. Maybe she had no other place to live. They'd stopped to rest before the last climb. It was cooler under the trees and they had a good visual field around them for a change and weren't worried about a close-in ambush.

Azalina had an open sore on her foot that Roca had noticed and he wiped it off with antiseptic and put a bandage on it to keep it clean.

He joked with Azalina about how he was going to get her a job as a scout in the Rangers, telling her she was a true warrior.

"You have warrior feet," he said.

"What's that?" She giggled, playing with her toes.

"Lots of calluses on the bottom. You can sneak around and nobody can hear you."

He gave her another PowerBar. Azalina thanked him, and Anna found herself finally warming to Roca. A little. Underneath that stiff, porcelain exterior, just maybe there was a human being after all.

Anna even got him to open up a little about his background. He told her that he grew up in a suburb of Baltimore, that he did his undergrad work at Towson University before getting his law degree at George Washington.

When they headed up the last leg of the journey toward the cave, they'd become a tight little team. Each one looking out for the other.

Maybe this was going to work, Anna thought. Maybe the worst is over. They were almost there. They had brought along a powerful field med-kit and she was well trained in handling all kinds of trauma.

At one of their pauses, she said hopefully, "That logging camp could be a landing zone. Maybe we can be out of here in a couple of hours."

"That would be nice," Roca said. "Depends on what shape Jason is in."

They followed Azalina through a thick copse of bamboo to the edge of the narrow ravine, more like a fissure in the volcanic rock. The bridge was flimsy looking, rope and bamboo, that was only about fifteen or twenty feet across—but the drop to the jungle floor below had to be a good hundred feet.

Anna turned and saw Roca staring at her. He smiled and she smiled back, like they were actually friends.

"That doesn't look all that safe," Roca announced with some trepidation.

"Yes. It's very strong," Azalina insisted. "I always go fast."

"You're what, sixty pounds?"

"It's okay," Azalina insisted. And it was. She went over first, followed by Anna, then Roca. The footbridge did a little swaying, some creaking and sagging, but it held.

Once the three of them were on the other side, Roca decided, since they'd be going north with Jason to find a landing zone, the bridge would serve no good purpose. "We need to cut this down. That'll make it impossible for anyone following us to get across."

Anna wasn't so sure. "If something goes wrong, maybe it would be a good idea to have a back door off this mountain. What if we run into some soldiers on the north side?"

"I don't think your father will be capable of running all over the place. Once we're committed, that's it. We'll just have to fight our way out if it comes to that."

He took out his K-Bar combat knife and hacked the thick rope cable on one side, and Anna, submitting to his logic, hacked away at the other side. It took them a few minutes to get through the thick, intertwined ropes, but they finally sent the bridge flapping across the chasm and hitting the rocks on the other side.

Now there was only one way out. Right through some of the biggest fires on the island.

But it was also where the old lava flows left some open spots in the jungle that might be big enough for choppers to get in. Anna had made note of the area before they'd left.

Azalina gathered some fruit on the way to the cave. She knew exactly where all the different fruits were located and called the one that looked like a pinkish-brown kiwi a *ciku.*

Anna tasted its soft, sweet flesh. Then Azalina handed her a jackfruit called *cempedak* and a banana she called *pisang mas.*

Roca's remark about Azalina being the perfect candidate for a Ranger scout seemed to have taken hold with her. She began to take an interest in their equipment, especially the helmets with the night-vision monocular and the built-in radio. She seemed so pleased and Anna could do nothing but smile at her eagerness.

On the last and most difficult climb up through rocks and then into thick bamboo, Anna began to wonder how she would react to seeing her father. And she began to deal with the possibility that he might not be alive.

Azalina stopped. "The cave is here."

Anna saw nothing that looked like a cave. Bamboo and trees grew in front of the heavy outcrop of granite walls.

Azalina grabbed Anna's hand. "This way."

Anna hesitated, her stomach beginning to churn up a bitter acid. She tried to suppress the emotions and wait until she knew what the situation was, but that proved impossible. Azalina kept pulling her forward. She felt a mixture of fear and excitement, and prayed that her father was alive, but she prepared for the worst at the same time.

"Wait here," Azalina said. Before Anna could stop her, the little girl vanished.

Roca, standing just behind Anna, said, "No wonder they couldn't find him. You okay?"

"Little nervous."

"Eight years is a long time."

She remembered her mother telling her a long time ago that her father was unhappy with a normal stable life. He had a need for ever-bigger adventures. He was always restless. Even long after their divorce, she never heard her mother say mean things about him the way some divorced women did about their ex-husbands.

And for the couple of years he was still in their life, they had never used Anna as a centerpiece in any of their differences. But he was always gone somewhere fighting fires, skiing some wilderness mountains or climbing. Maybe it was just in the Quick gene pool.

His family traced their roots all the way back to the pioneers: mountain men, Indian fighters, silver miners. "You're a lot like him," her mother would say, always with a chagrined smile. Anna desperately wanted to see him.

Yes, Anna thought, she was a lot like him. The leaf didn't fall far from the tree.

Anna moved closer to the granite walls, her anxiety rising with each step. Maybe he wouldn't be anything like she remembered. Maybe this new world of his, and the tragedies that had befallen him, had turned him into somebody she wouldn't even recognize.

But he's still my father, no matter what, she said to herself. Nothing can change that.

There, beneath a tangle of jungle vines, waiting to see him come out, she heard Azalina scream.

It was a terrible wail that sent shivers through Anna.

Before she could get to the entrance, Azalina came running screaming, tears in her eyes.

Oh my God, Anna thought. *He's dead.*

Part Four
Operation Fierce Snake

Chapter 18

Azalina, hysterically crying, tried to run off.

Anna grabbed her. "Stay here. Don't run away." Azalina fought her like a little tiger, yelling in Malay, crying as Anna struggled to restrain and calm her.

Roca went into the cave and returned a few seconds later. "He's not dead, he's gone."

"The terrorists took him! They'll kill him!" Azalina screamed, tears flowing down her face. "They'll put him on television and cut off his head."

"Shut her up," Roca said. "They'll hear us for miles."

Anna struggled to muffle Azalina's explosion of grief, telling her over and over that Jason wasn't dead, that he was probably just wandering around and they'd find him.

In the midst of this hysteria there was a single gunshot—and it wasn't far away. Then they heard a wild voice yelling some incoherent epithet.

Azalina stopped sobbing instantly. She tore away from Anna and raced off into the thicket of bamboo yelling in Malay: *"Dadah! Dadah!"*

Anna took off after her. She heard Roca swearing behind her. They crashed through the bamboo and then the heavy underbrush for about a hundred yards.

When Anna reached Azalina she saw her father. He was standing by a narrow, fast little waterfall waving a gun, his eyes wide and wild looking.

Oh God, Anna thought, he looks crazy. She immediately thought of Joseph Conrad's character Kurtz in his famous novel *Heart of Darkness*.

Jason wore nothing but cotton shorts and he was a mess of skin welts. His leg was bandaged but the bandages were coming off, revealing an ugly wound. His upper body glistened with sweat, and he had a scraggly beard and matted hair.

"Dad," Anna said quietly. "It's Anna."

He didn't respond and didn't stop yelling at some phantom in the jungle.

Anna walked up to him.

He pointed the gun at her, his eyes wild.

"Are you going to shoot your daughter? It's Anna, Dad. You sent for me, remember? To get you out of here."

He kept trying to focus on her. Finally he got it. "Anna?"

"Yes, it's Anna."

"Anna! Anna!" He took two steps toward her and collapsed.

Azalina let out a little whimper of a scream and ran to his side yelling, "*Dadah! Dadah!* You can't die! You can't die!"

Anna dropped beside her father. His pulse was fast and his breathing was erratic but strong. He was suffering from an intense fever.

"Let's get him back to the cave. Azalina, the cave is cooler than outside, isn't it?"

"Yes."

"You have water?"

"Yes."

It took all three of them to carry Jason back to the cave. They got him inside on his makeshift bed at the rear of the narrow room.

Anna looked around her father's hideout after she and Azalina got him to lie on a small bamboo-and-burlap bed.

A flickering light from an oil lamp that sat on a bamboo table barely gave off enough light to see anything clearly, or perhaps her eyes simply hadn't adjusted to the dimness of the cave.

Jason was sweating and felt hot to the touch. Anna pulled her pack off, put it on the rocky floor and began to dig out the medical kit. She sat on a short wooden stool next to his bed.

"We need to get some fluids and antibiotics into him," she told Azalina. "Can you get me some water?"

"Yes. There's plenty of water." She pulled a plastic gallon container from under the table.

Anna said, "Is that good water?"

"Yes. I get it from the springs."

Azalina produced a coconut-shell cup.

While that was going on, Roca was making a systematic and somewhat frantic search of the cave.

"Where the hell is it? There's no laptop here," Roca cried in exasperation.

"Maybe there isn't any laptop at all," Anna suggested.

With Azalina's help, she managed to get some water into her father. He kept staring at her as if trying to figure out who she was.

Then suddenly it came to him. His mind seemed to clear. "Anna?"

"Yes, it's Anna."

"Oh, my God, Anna. Baby."

"It's so good to see you, Daddy. You're a mess."

"I am. I'm a terrible mess. It's so good to see you. I don't understand. What are you doing here? Oh, yes, yes. Good. I knew you'd come."

Anna was stunned by how frail and weak he was. "I came to get you out of here. Get you to a doctor."

Jason turned from Anna now, glanced at Roca, a look of confusion coming over him. He turned back to Anna. "Where's John Brock?"

"He didn't come."

"Who's that?"

"Tom Roca."

"What the hell is he doing here? I told them to send Brock."

"Dad, calm down. I need to clean your wounds and get some antibiotics into you and more water. Don't worry about Roca. He just wants to look at the laptop. Do you have the laptop?"

"I'm not giving that to anybody but Brock. All these other bastards, you can't trust them. You should have brought Brock."

The Hammond

Brock gave DeAngelo a look. "A little girl?"

"That's what Roca says."

"Island girl?"

"Didn't say. A Malay girl around nine or ten years old. Speaks perfect English. She's was stalking them for some time, and finally came forward. Identified herself as the guide who was going to take them to Jason."

"Did she?"

"Yeah. They found him. Not in good shape. Maybe out of his mind. They found him running around in the jungle with nothing on but shorts, waving a gun."

"Shit."

"Yeah, he nearly shot his daughter."

"Great," Brock said, shaking his head in dismay. "This just gets better and better." He knew he shouldn't have been surprised.

DeAngelo shrugged.

Swartzlander, who walked up next to DeAngelo, said, "You gotta love this. We got a little girl guiding a CIA desk jockey, a madman and a civilian female fire-fighter in a deadly environment that right now might just be the most hostile piece of real estate in the Pacific."

"A job's a job," Brock said.

Swartzlander shook his head. "You just can't let the—" he lowered his voice "—spooks play soldier. Never works. Just gets people killed."

Brock heard Swartzlander, but his mind was elsewhere. New intercepts were coming in constantly, and they indicated increased radio traffic among the hostile forces combing the island.

Things were going downhill fast.

Brock talked to Roca on the Sat phone and told him about the increased activity and urged him to get Jason Quick and move north where there was a possible landing zone in the lava fields.

The ship was now deep into the Malacca Strait, less than forty miles from the island. They could get a chopper in there in about twenty minutes.

He went into the communications room to see the updates from the drone they had sent in to check for possible landing sites.

Brock stared at the digital display of the location of the intercepts and the location of the transponders.

"One hell of a lot of activity all of a sudden," DeAngelo said.

Brock nodded. He didn't like what he was seeing. The hostile forces seemed to have a very good idea where Roca and Anna were. Their movements tightened on the mountain.

"We need to get them the hell out of there soon," Brock said. "This is going to heat up real fast."

"They're not going back to that logging camp,"

Swartzlander opined. "That doesn't leave any good options except north. And going north looks hazardous to their health."

And there was nothing anybody could do to help. They were on their own. But the drone was sending back some pictures of the lava fields in the north end of the island and they were promising landing-zone potential. That is, *if* their people could get to them. And that was looking like a very big if at the moment.

Even without the fires and dense layers of smoke, choppers were all but useless against small units of guerrillas protected by two-hundred-foot canopies. They couldn't find them and even if they did, they couldn't kill them.

Brock's frustration levels were peaking. He'd been on two busted operations in his career. They were bloody messes and he had no desire to add a third to his bio.

He glanced at Verrill who was talking to the ship's commander. If we go down in flames, he thought, I'm not letting you skate home free. I'll run this one all the way up the SOCOM's flagpole.

Chapter 19

Jason seemed to react fast to the introduction of fluids. His eyes cleared and he began to talk coherently.

"Dad, how long have you had this fever?"

"I don't know. A couple days, maybe. I can't remember when it started."

She felt much better about his chances now. Whatever he had, the antibiotic concoction was hitting it hard and fast.

Anna got some more water. "You need to sit up and drink some more."

He followed her instructions, but it was hard for him to pull himself up. Azalina helped while Anna held the cup. He took a few sips, swallowed the pill that Anna gave him and then had to lie back down.

"I knew you'd come."

"You need to drink more water, Dad."

"In a minute. I'm tired. I need to rest a second." He closed his eyes.

Anna's eyes finally adjusted to the dimness of the cave and she noticed several small open pots, a wicker basket and two wooden bowls sitting on the table not far from the bed. There were a few black notebooks and an assortment of pens and pencils also sitting on the table. The cave was almost empty except for several cans of soup, a stack of torn blankets and some tattered clothes along the far wall. The cave was narrow, maybe eight feet wide and about fifteen feet in depth. The ceiling was high enough in the center for an average-size person to stand. It looked like a medieval prison cell instead of a hideout.

Roca had gone out to look around. Now he came back in. "Jason, we have to get moving. Where's the laptop?"

Jason opened his eyes and stared at the cave ceiling. "The hell with Verrill."

"Anna, can you get through to him?"

Anna turned to her father. "Dad, if you have a laptop, we really do need it and then we have to go."

"They got to you, didn't they?"

"No, they didn't get to me. Dad—"

"They get to everybody sooner or later, the bastards."

Her heart was breaking seeing her father in such a weak and confused condition.

He seemed to slip away for a moment, lying back on Azalina's lap as she mopped his head with a rag.

Roca walked up next to Anna. "All that noise has pinpointed us. It won't take them long to get here. We're not leaving without that laptop. Get him to tell you where it is."

"I'll get it. You just upset him. Go outside, please."

Roca turned to Azalina. "You know where it is, don't you, Azalina."

"You go to hell," Jason said, trying to sit up. "Leave her out of this."

Anna motioned for Roca to leave, and pushed her dad back toward the bed.

When the CIA agent was gone, Jason started rambling about secrets and people who were getting killed because of Verrill. Anna couldn't make much sense out of any of it. "Dad," she said, "I'm going to clean your wounds and put new bandages on."

Anna removed the bandages. What she saw, and smelled, was the beginning of a serious infection. The entry was on the outside of the left thigh, nasty and blackened. An even bigger exit wound was underneath. The bullet had apparently not destroyed the bone or he wouldn't be able to walk at all, and his whole thigh would have been much more swollen.

Anna reached for antiseptic and some pads. "Azalina, did you do this?"

"Yes. But he tears at the bandages."

"It's very good. You did a nice job."

Azalina nodded with a glow of pride.

Jason muttered his thanks and squeezed Azalina's arm. He spoke to her in a Malay dialect and she answered in the same dialect. He nodded and pushed himself up to get another drink of water. This time Azalina helped him with the cup.

Anna wiped down the wound and began to rebandage it.

He rambled about his connection in Kuala Lumpur and Singapore and about everybody being dead. She finished with the bandaging but was worried about the wound. It looked like a staph infection. "Dad, we need to get you to a hospital. If gangrene sets in, you could lose your leg."

Azalina brought him more water.

Jason fell back on a pile of tattered T-shirts that functioned as a pillow. Azalina continued to wipe the sweat from his forehead, and for the next twenty minutes or so he slipped into another bout of delirium. Anna was scared. Whatever had a hold of him wasn't as easy to beat back as she'd thought just a few minutes ago.

Her dad was like a man caught up in a nightmare, yelling crazy things in Malay or Chinese, she didn't know which. He almost came off the bed several times and would have if Anna and Azalina hadn't stopped him.

Anna got him calmed down. She turned to Azalina. "You called him *Dadah*. What does that mean in English?"

"Dad."

Anna stared at her. "Azalina, is Jason…is he…is he your *father*?"

Azalina nodded. "Yes."

"Your *real* father?"

"Yes. My real father. You're my half sister."

It was another shock, but this time a very pleasant one. And one that finally explained to Anna why he'd wanted her to come here.

But she was still confused. "I thought...I thought that the tsunami took his whole family. That's what they told me."

"It took my mom and my two brothers and my cousins and...everyone else. It took the whole village. But Dad and I were in town. We were saved. He says we were saved for a special purpose. That God spares those he needs for some special purpose. That's why I have to be strong. Someday when I grow up, I'll find my special purpose."

"Yes, you will. And he's right. You will find that great purpose."

Anna could hardly digest all that was coming at her. For a moment she just stared at the little girl who was the sister that she didn't know she had. This little girl who was dealing with tragedies and circumstances unimaginable, and yet somehow had, incredibly, been able to keep herself together. Keep herself strong. That was definitely something she got from her father.

"I'm very happy that you are my sister," Anna said. "And *my* mom is going to love you. Oh, is she going to love you."

Azalina lit up. "I will be very glad to meet her. And I have your picture."

"You do?"

"Yes. Our house was destroyed, but Dad had a small

safe that was fire- and waterproof. We found it and I saved some pictures. Dad thinks you are the greatest smoke jumper and soccer player in all the world. He told me lots of stories."

"I'm sure he exaggerates a little bit."

They talked for a few more minutes. Anna was just amazed at how open Azalina was. Then Anna said, "We really do have to get moving. Is there a laptop?"

– "Yes."

"Do you know where it is?"

"Yes. It's near where we found him. The waterfall. Between the rocks, in a hole there."

"We need to get it."

"Those bastards!" Jason sat up.

"Dad, relax. Lie down."

"No. Listen to me."

"What?"

He grabbed her and pulled her close. He smelled horrible, his breath was sickeningly sweet. He dug his fingers into her arm and whispered harshly into her ear, "You have to promise me."

"What?"

"They're going to kill me."

"Who is?"

"They're going to kill me."

"Dad, nobody is going to kill you."

She gently removed his hand. "Lie down and rest. We need you to be strong."

He resisted for a moment, then finally relented and laid back and stared up and mumbled in Malay.

Anna got up and motioned Azalina to come with her away from their father.

She whispered to her, "Can you take me to the laptop?"

Azalina glanced at her father, then said, "Yes."

"We have to get it. It's very important. It might save thousands of lives. And we can't take him to a hospital until we get it. Do you understand?"

"Yes. I'll take you there."

She said to Roca as they passed him as they left the cave, "I'm going to get the laptop. Watch him."

"Where is it?"

"It's not very far."

"Maybe I should go with Azalina," Roca suggested. "You can stay here with your father."

"No. You stay here. I'll be right back. And don't aggravate him."

Chapter 20

Azalina led Anna back to the narrow waterfall. She went up into the outcrops of volcanic rock. It was cool there and she stared at the pool of water and wanted nothing more in the world than to strip off her stinky clothes, jump in and just wallow.

Unfortunately, she thought with deep chagrin, that was not going to be possible.

"It's up there, in the rocks," Azalina said. Then she turned to Anna. "Will Dad be angry with me?"

"No. Not really. He can't think clearly right now with the fever he has. And we need to get him out of here, and the laptop has to go to Roca before we can leave."

Azalina nodded. "Okay." She stared up into the rocks.

"Be careful of snakes," Anna said reflexively, though she knew that Azalina was undoubtedly ten times as aware of her surroundings as any outsider could be.

"I'm okay," Azalina said.

Anna wished she had time to sit and talk. There was so much she wanted to know about Azalina, her brothers and mother, the world she came from.

The resiliency of humans never ceased to amaze her. What they endured. She only wished she had half their strength and willpower.

Azalina disappeared in the rocks, then reappeared with a thin laptop in a blue metal case. She waved and Anna waved back.

She watched her sister come down without so much as a missed step, her little feet grabbing footholds with sureness.

Azalina cradled the laptop and brought it to her.

On their way back to the cave, Azalina stopped and pointed. Anna couldn't see anything at first. She took out her binoculars and scanned the forest below. Finally she found them. A string of guerrilla soldiers moving across a clearing. Then they vanished into the forest.

"How long will it take them to get up here?" Anna asked.

"I thought it would be a lot longer with the bridge gone. Now, I don't know."

Just before she and Anna reached the cave, Azalina turned to her. "When we go to America, can we go on the *Star Wars* ride in Disneyland?"

"Sure. Is that your favorite movie?"

"Uh-huh."

"And can you teach me to be a smoke jumper?"

"I'll teach you anything you want to learn. You'll have to be a little older, though, to be a smoke jumper."

"Is Mr. Roca your boyfriend?"

"No. He's just…he's helping us."

"How old do you have to be to become a Ranger scout?"

"Probably around twenty."

Satisfied, Azalina started off.

Anna peered through a break in the trees and got a glimpse of some new fires to the north. She wondered if the men after them were deliberately setting the fires, trying to trap them on the mountain.

There was no open flat ground for the choppers to land. And with pirate boats patrolling the island like circling sharks, getting to the water, even if they could, would be of little help. Choppers were the only way out and that was looking like a smaller and smaller window of opportunity. Anna knew getting her dad off this mountain was going to be an enormous challenge.

She ducked into the cave carrying the laptop.

Roca was reading one of the black notebooks by the light of the oil lamp. Her father was asleep and his breathing was raspy and irregular.

"Ah, great," he whispered, taking the computer from her.

"Are those my dad's?" she asked, pointing to the notebooks, a little put off by Roca's reading what she thought were her father's private journals.

"Yes. They're his and they can't get into the hands of the terrorists. I'm surprised he'd put down on paper some of his thoughts about the trade. In this business, you don't want any kind of trails, paper or otherwise.

"Anna, get your father ready to go in about fifteen minutes. It'll take me that long to run a program. I hope there's battery life." He took a CD out of his backpack. "This baby can break just about any code that's on here."

"He's going to need walking sticks," Anna said. "Azalina, you want to help me?"

They went out and selected a young piece of bamboo from the thicket. The wood proved extremely hard to cut. Azalina showed her the right way so it wouldn't splinter or shred.

When they got back, Anna glanced over at Roca as he sat on the ground watching the screen. "Anything?"

"Not yet."

"If it's in Malay, can you read it? Because, Azalina—"

"I'm very familiar with Malay," Roca shot back curtly. "It's called Bahasa in Malaysia. Indonesia has its version they call Bahasa Indonesian. They are very similar."

Anna got a peek at something coming up on the screen. Good, she thought. Maybe Dad isn't as crazy as he seems.

Anna and Azalina finished the walking sticks in the cave. Jason was sleeping fitfully. Her father was in a rambling delirium, again talking nonsensically about something, hands waving, voice mumbling, sighing.

Anna rebandaged the wounded left leg, wrapping it tighter this time to help him walk easier. With Azalina's help, she also got him to swallow a strong dose of Vicodin.

She went through his pack to see what might be worth taking. She found a plastic folder with a bunch of pictures. Azalina pointed out pictures of Anna. In one of them she was about Azalina's age. The rest were of Azalina, her mother, brothers and some of her other relatives.

Anna stared at them for a few minutes, then put them back in the plastic folder and into her pack. She couldn't deal with all her emotions right now and what the pictures represented to her.

Her father's only weapon was a small .32-caliber pistol. She put that in her pack as well along with his journals. That was it. A decade of his life was now reduced to just a few pictures, some notebooks, a gun and a daughter.

Her father's fever seemed to have spiked over the past few minutes. She tried to cool him down but the water was too warm and there was nothing to do but watch and hope that the medicines she'd gotten into him would help.

Then he seemed suddenly to relax. He opened his eyes and smiled, as if he'd just seen her for the first time. "Anna. Anna you came. I knew you'd come."

"Yes, Dad. I'm here." She took his hand.

"They told me about you, what you were doing. I was very proud."

"Thanks."

He gripped her hand tighter. Tears came to his eyes. "I lost my boys. My beautiful boys. I lost them, Anna.

The sea took them and it took my sweet wife. My Seri." Tears rolled from his eyes. "So many died. So many."

Anna cried with him, for the stepmother she never knew and the brothers she would never get to meet. She cried for all the pain and sorrow he must have gone through, and was still experiencing.

He was silent for a time. Then he looked at her with bloodshot eyes, shook his head sadly, and his mind seemed to push all the horror away.

He choked and coughed and Azalina gave him more water. "She is my salvation," he said, squeezing Azalina's hand. "Without her I wouldn't have made it this far."

When he had finished drinking, he handed her the cup. "How's your mother, Anna?"

"She's fine. She's running her own outfitter business now."

"She ever remarry?"

"No. She's too busy."

"Yes, that's her."

He smiled. "Anna, you see now why I wanted you here. I didn't think I could make it and I needed you to get your sister—"

"Don't say that," Azalina scolded.

"I'm sorry. Just in case. She is a trouper." He smiled at Azalina. "She outwits the soldiers, brings me food and water. She even stole some medicine from the camps. The pirates and jihadists are no match for her."

Anna said, "Dad, we need you to be able to walk. I'm going to give you something that will help your energy and some painkillers so you won't have so much trouble." She pulled out one of Brock's pills. "It should help you stay awake."

"I much prefer herbal remedies," Jason said. "I took the Vicodin. I'm not taking anything else."

"You're going back to the States, so you might as well get back into Western-style pill popping."

He smiled. "I miss your acerbic humor. And no, I'm not getting into pill popping."

"By the way, Dad, where were the letters explaining your absence?"

"I wasn't allowed to risk it. But I was always under the assumption you were told something."

"Well, I wasn't."

"Anna, I'm so sorry. I didn't know." Taking her hand, he said, "Listen carefully, I'll give *you* the laptop. You make sure it goes to Brock. Don't trust anyone else."

"Dad, I can't do that. I'm not authorized to get involved in anything but getting you, and now Azalina, out. Roca has the laptop. We had to give it to him so we can get out of here. He wasn't leaving without it."

Her father shook his head slowly, in surrender. "Yes, you're right. You don't have the authority. And you're right, it's just like them to make it a condition of letting us go. If that's their intention at all."

"You have to stop this now," Anna said. "You're scaring Azalina. You make no sense. I want you to listen to me. Complain all you want once we're out of here, but not now. Okay."

"Where is Roca?"

"He's outside decoding the computer."

"You better make sure he's out there. Maybe he just took off."

"He didn't take off."

"How do you know that? You can't trust these people. I know them."

Anna smiled. "He didn't take off, because without help he wouldn't get far. He's just not that much of an off-road kind of guy."

Jason chuckled. Then he grabbed her arm and said, "If you gave him the computer, then you have to at least do one thing for me. I don't care how whacked-out paranoid you think I am. And I'm sure I'm a little nuts. Maybe even a lot more than a little. But I'm not completely gone, Anna. I hope."

"What is it?"

He reached under the mats and came out with a tiny device that she recognized instantly as a JumpDrive memory stick. The one he had in his hand, not even as big as his thumb, could hold a ton of data. She, and just about everyone she knew who feared losing files, downloaded them onto these portable drives. He handed it to her. "Put this in one of your pockets, say nothing about it, and when you see Brock, give it to him. Promise me you'll do that."

"I promise."

She had several small inside pockets that had water-sealed zippers. She slipped the JumpDrive into her pocket. She didn't want to get into a discussion with him as to why he was so fearful of his own people. She just wanted to get the hell out of there.

"Azalina, go see if Roca's still with us," Jason said.

Azalina jumped up and went outside.

Jason grabbed Anna's hand again. "I couldn't get back. When I heard about the first wave, I left Azalina with a friend and took a motorcycle. I didn't get back! The roads were clogged! Everything was total chaos! It was a nightmare!" Tears filled his eyes. She wanted to stop him, but he insisted on continuing.

She kept flashing back to the TV coverage and trying to integrate the horror story he was telling her, the endless days and weeks of searching, never finding the bodies, and having to try to make sense out of it all to Azalina. And then the trouble began with his secret work. The long downhill slide.

Anna was almost glad when Azalina returned.

Until she said, "He's not outside. He went out by the ridge."

"Did you say anything to him?" Anna asked.

She shook her head. "He was looking with his binoculars. I didn't bother him."

"Where's the laptop?" Jason asked.

"I didn't see it."

"You stay with your father and help him get dressed," Anna said. "Is Roca straight out through the bamboo, the way we came in?"

"Yes."

Chapter 21

Anna pushed through the thicket of bamboo to the ridgeline and saw Roca there with binoculars scanning the world below from the cover of a tree.

"Anything moving around down there?"

"Yes. Two groups of soldiers working their way up. I'd say they're still an hour away. It's a hard climb coming that way."

"How's the program working? I didn't see the laptop."

Roca turned and walked back to her. He shook his head. "Not a damn thing on it."

Anna stared at him. "Are you serious? Nothing?"

"Zip." He put the glasses away. "The files are gone. If they ever existed."

"Maybe you just couldn't get in."

"Believe me. The computer was clean. Nothing in backup or the recycle bin. If there ever was anything on there, it's been expertly cleaned. I'm not sure there ever was anything on it."

Anna could've sworn that when she glanced over on her way into the cave, she saw something on the screen. She was almost sure of it. But he was saying there was absolutely nothing. How could that be?

Anna thought it was probably just one of those things where she expected to see something, so she thought she did when she didn't. Still, it was enough to make her second-guess herself. If the laptop was empty, it was empty.

"Where is it?"

"Somewhere down there." He indicated the drop to the jungle below. "Not much sense in lugging it back with us." Changing the subject quickly, he asked, "Is he ready to go?"

Roca's blasé attitude toward the laptop annoyed her. "Azalina is helping him get dressed. Are you sure the computer had nothing? Sometimes, even after everything is erased, there are ways—"

He folded his arms around his weapon as if cradling it and said, "Believe me, there's no way. Computers are my specialty. It's as empty as a politician's promise. I'm afraid all your father wanted was to be sure Azalina got out. She's the only survivor in his Malaysian family from the tsunami. You had some time with him. He coherent at all?"

"Better."

"Now you understand why I'm here," Roca said.

"Not just for the laptop, but because we didn't know your father's condition. When an agent goes over the edge you never know what you're facing. We've had disturbing reports for some time. Agents in the field, especially in deep cover, sometimes go native. But your father, whatever else his problems are, has also suffered some unbelievable trauma. I'm experienced in handling this kind of thing. Brock isn't. He's a soldier. Jason is one of ours and we like to handle our own. What has he been telling you?"

"Nothing. He talks about my childhood." She lied but didn't care. Her father had suffered enough. She felt sad for her father and all the trauma he'd suffered in the past year. And she didn't want Roca interrogating him in his current state.

Roca became almost overly sympathetic. "It's really unfortunate. He was a top agent. One of the very best. It happens. The tsunami tragedy…nobody can deal with all of that. It's just too much. The last thing he could hold on to over here was Azalina. And I'm sure he was carrying a load of guilt about not being there when the waves hit. That's a terrible burden."

Anna walked over to look down the hill at where he said the soldiers were and was met almost instantly by a burst of gunfire from below. She dodged quickly back from the precipice.

"I think that's a message that it's time to boogie," Roca said.

They raced back to the cave.

Roca stayed outside. "Get Jason and Azalina. I'll let

the extraction team know we're on the move." He took out his SAT phone.

The Hammond

Brock ordered his team to get ready to go the minute he got the report that Roca and Anna had Jason Quick and his other daughter in tow were on the move and being pursued. Roca then shocked everybody when he reported that the laptop was empty, that it had been a ruse to get Quick's Malaysian daughter out. He also said he didn't know if Quick would be able to make it. He was too sick and weak. Roca told them that he was going to try to get the daughters to leave him, but he wasn't sure if he could.

Brock hated everything he was hearing. "What's the flight time?"

"From our current position, about twenty minutes," DeAngelo said, "if we had a landing zone. Which, as of right now, we don't. They're moving in the direction of the lava field. That's the best bet. If they can get there."

"That's tough terrain and we'll intercept a lot of chatter from hostile forces," Brock warned.

Swartzlander, who was plotting the movement of the fires, said, "They might have more to worry about with this fire that's moving quickly than with the guerrilla fighters chasing them. That damn thing is exploding up that mountain."

Without the laptop, they had nothing. If, and now it was a big *if,* there was a ship out there with dangerous cargo, they now had no way of knowing what ship, where it was or its destination. Brock imagined a ship with special cargo containers carrying deadly uranium pulling into some port, defeating the normal detection procedures, being loading onto a different, unknown ship...

Operation Fierce Snake was turning into a total disaster.

Chapter 22

Pouco Vulcao Island

"We need to get out of here," Anna said.

"How close?" Jason asked.

"It's hard to tell how long it will take them to get up here, but they can't be more than two or three hundred yards below us."

Azalina brought the walking sticks over to her father's bed. Anna helped him up. He grabbed the bamboo sticks and took a few tentative steps.

"How does the leg feel?" Anna asked.

"With all that Vicodin in me, I could probably climb Everest. Where's Roca?"

"Outside."

"The laptop?"

"Empty."

He gave her a look, then shook his head as if there was really never any doubt in his mind that it would be empty. "Of course."

"You didn't just use that as an excuse—"

"No. I would do pretty much anything to get her out of here—" he glanced at Azalina "—but I would have gone about it differently. The laptop was loaded, believe me." His face calmed and he took a step toward Anna. "Baby, you made me a promise and I want you to keep it."

"I will."

Whether her father was delusional was up in the air with her now. She'd finally come to realize that in this murky subterranean world of Special Ops, CIA and undercover agents, nothing was as it seemed.

Just then Roca barged in. "What's going on? What promise?"

"Nothing!" Jason snapped. "Mind your own damn business."

"Why are we wasting time? Lets get out of here," Anna stated. "We've stayed way too long already."

Roca stared at her for an intense moment, as if he wasn't ready to buy it. He glanced at Jason. "What's this about a promise?"

"Whatever it is," Jason said, "it doesn't concern you."

Obviously annoyed, Roca turned and walked out. They followed Roca outside and through the bamboo to the ridgeline. Azalina took over from there, leading them in the opposite direction from which they'd come in. Roca followed her and then Jason. Anna stayed behind him in case he faltered. He was an expert with hiking poles and that was a big plus.

Anna recalled what her father was once like—the flow of waves in his hair, the smell of his aftershave, and how thrilled she was to be so important to him that he wanted to teach her everything.

And now, dressed in his ragged clothes, his face gaunt and ruddy, his gray hair matted as he leaned over to rest after only a few steps, he didn't smell of aftershave, he smelled of sweat and dirt and the topical antibiotics she'd applied to his wounds.

But to Anna he would always be that dad teaching her about cougar tracks, the same Dad no matter how wounded, or how sick. It just made her sad to see him this way. To see him battling for his life, the drawn skin, the sunken eyes, the long hard breaths. She saw the struggle in him and a panic, not for himself, but for them, his daughters, his legacy. And maybe for everyone else caught up in this tragic war.

They worked their way along the ridgeline, Jason forcing the pace to a steady crawl. It was difficult and slow going and Anna had to keep a hand on Jason at times to steady him. He still used the trekking poles like second legs.

In the growing twilight, voices from below filtered up through the trees. The soldiers were closing the gap and fast—but darkness would slow them down.

The winds changed again. Anna could hear the roar

and feel the heat of the fires. She had gotten them in, now she put her faith in Brock to get them out.

Her father stumbled and Anna grabbed him. This time she held his arm and wouldn't let him go. He didn't fight her. So many times in their hikes when she was little he'd help her up difficult terrain, always smiling at her. Sometimes he'd just hoist her up on his shoulders and carry her for miles. He was so strong in the mountains then, and now he wasn't. Now it was her turn.

When Azalina glanced back, Anna could see the apprehension in her eyes, the furtive fears that meant they were in big trouble.

Suddenly Azalina froze. She made a motion with her hand to get down. Anna and Jason sank to their haunches, then their knees. Anna kept one hand on her weapon. Roca went up ahead with Azalina.

Time reduced itself to near absolute zero. Nothing moved but her blood. Crouched, hiding, listening, waiting for life or death to claim them. Anna didn't doubt that they would have to fight their way out sooner or later. Too many guerrilla soldiers were looking for them. At its most primitive, most basic, this is what life is, she thought. All animals face it. They kill to survive.

She peered into the deepening gloom, pulling down the night-vision monocular. Her mouth was dry, her chest tight, her stomach cold. This wasn't like any other fear she'd ever had.

Finally the voices slowly faded as the men climbed toward the cave.

Anna had sensed that Azalina had led their small

team in the wrong direction to get down the mountain, but apparently she'd done it purposely to avoid the soldiers and it had worked. The child was brilliant. Their dad had taught her well.

Then Azalina gave them the signal to move again. The lack of trails made it difficult. Difficult and slow. They sidehilled just below a ridge for a long time, then cut down into a gorge where they found a narrow animal trail. They followed it into the evening, constantly stopping to rest and listen.

"How are you doing?" Anna asked her father.

He nodded, smiled, but it was a painful smile. She could tell he was already exhausted, and she began to worry about his ability to walk all the way to the landing zone. But she was determined to get him out, alive, no matter how long it took, and no matter what difficulty might come their way.

Her father was going home.

The Hammond

Once Brock's team knew the direction of Roca's descent, they'd sent a drone earlier over the island. It sent back pictures of possible landing zones and Brock decided on one in particular that would work. He'd reported the coordinates to Roca. Now it was only a question of time. Roca's team had to reach the LZ under the cover of darkness. Luckily with Jason so hurt, they were moving slower than they had originally planned.

Brock stared at the latest intercepts being automatically translated on the screen from the hostile units on the island. In spite of the fires, the Mujahideen were flooding the place. Boats filled with soldiers arrived at different locations every hour.

They seemed to know exactly where their quarry was and they were closing in fast.

Finally Brock ordered his men to mount up, the choppers readied for takeoff. He wasn't only worried about the guerrilla fighters, he was also worried about the truth behind this operation.

He refused to believe there was nothing on that laptop, not with all the activity on the ground. And he knew Jason's history and character well enough to know that even if the man was delirious and even dying, and all he wanted was to get his kid out, he would never fake something this big to do it. The man would have found another way.

But Brock couldn't figure it out. Couldn't figure out what war game Roca was playing. He could only hope the man would do everything in his power to get Anna and her family out. Nothing short of that would be acceptable.

Brock went up on the deck. The pilots were running their checklists. His team was saddling up. They were the best in the business. The best on the face of this earth, as far as he was concerned. He didn't have to give them any pep talk. They knew their job. Once in, they wouldn't come back without the people they had gone in for.

Chapter 23

Pouco Vulcao Island

They broke out of heavy growth and were forced to stop at the base of a granite shelf that looked at least fifteen feet high. Vines offered some climbing possibilities, but Anna could see that it was going to be difficult to get her father up and over.

She was thinking about using some nylon rope to put under his arms and then having Roca get up top to pull, while she and Azalina helped him climb, but Roca came towards her with another idea. "Jason is completely spent. He's going to have to stay."

"What? No! He'll make it."

"We can't get him over this."

"We'll get him wherever we have to!" Anna shot back.

Roca shook his head. "Even if we could, he'll be too weak to make it the rest of the way. We're going to have to leave him here and bring in a ground team."

"How far are we from the landing zone?"

"Close."

"Then we can take him."

"No. The choppers are already on their way. I'll go on ahead and meet them. You, your dad and Azalina stay right here and wait for me. This is a good spot to defend yourself if you have to."

Anna looked at her father. "I can make it," he said, looking up the face of the climb. "Let's go."

"You're not going to even try. I don't want you to take the risk," Roca said. "If you fall, it'll just make things that much worse. We'll come back for you."

"You're lying," Jason protested. "You have no intention of sending a team back for us."

Anna ignored her father and urged Roca to change his mind. The fires were too close for them to stay where they were. With the trajectory of the wind, the flames could be on them within a couple hours—if the guerrillas didn't get to them first.

"My dad's one of the best climbers I've ever seen. He has great upper-body strength. He can make it if we help him."

"No time. He'll slow us down," Roca argued. "Stay here and stay low. I'll be back with a combat team."

"He's lying," Jason said again. "At least take my

daughters with you. I don't care if you leave me, but don't leave them. They're *innocent* in all of this."

Anna couldn't deal with this constant battle between her father and Roca. This wasn't a good place to start yelling and screaming. She could see Roca had no intention of backing down. And as long as Brock was on the boat, there was no way they'd be left behind. She decided to let Roca go, then she'd figure out how to get her father up and over the steep bank.

"Dad, they'll come for us. Roca, go on. We'll take care of ourselves."

She had her own doubts about the situation, but decided she had no choice but to do it herself. It was inconceivable to her that Brock would abandon them. But then, she reflected, what did she really know about Brock? Maybe he was just very good at concealing the truth. What did she know about anything where these people were concerned?

"No," Jason insisted. "You and your sister go with him. I'll wait here. Just leave me a weapon. Roca, I'm begging you, get my daughters out of here."

"They won't leave you," Roca said. "Do what Anna tells you to do."

Roca turned to survey how he was going to climb up the steep bank of rock but couldn't come up with a good plan. He tried to discuss it with Azalina, but she refused.

"If you can help him, it'll get us out of here faster," Anna said, urging her sister to help.

Azalina gave in and told Roca how he should work with the roots, which ones to grab and which ones not to grab because they were either thorny or slippery.

Roca seemed very impressed. "Thanks," he told her. "You will one day become a great Ranger scout."

"You'll hurry and be back to get us."

He smiled down at her. "Don't worry. I will."

"You have to," Azalina said, a worried look on her face. "If you don't, Anna won't get the JumpDri-"

"Azalina!" Jason yelled. "Be quiet. Let him go."

But Roca didn't leave.

He stared at Azalina for a second. Suddenly he turned to Anna with a look of concern on his face. "Anna, what is she talking about?"

"I don't know. She just wants to make sure you'll come back."

"Yeah, right," Roca said. "Let's stop the games. I take it you have a JumpDrive. Hand it over."

"Don't give him anything, Anna," Jason demanded angrily.

She thought about the memory stick weighing heavily in her pocket and the questions she had about what Roca did with the laptop now leaped to the forefront of her mind.

Roca glared at Anna. "How stupid do you want to play this? You're here to get your family out."

"Anna, don't listen—"

"Dad, let me handle this."

"Anna," Roca warned, his eyes tightening, "If you don't hand that over real soon, I'm not sure how this will play out. But it won't be good."

"Anna," Jason yelled.

Roca turned to Azalina. "You know I want to get

your father and sister out of here, but I think they're hiding something from me. It could be very important. You were—"

"Leave her alone," Jason demanded. "Azalina, come over here."

"We're making a lot of noise," Azalina said, walking over to her dad. "The soldiers will hear us. Mr. Roca has to hurry, Daddy." Fear welled up on her face.

Azalina continued, her voice cracking, "You have to let him go meet the people in the helicopters so they can come back and get us. You have to!"

"Baby, you don't understand," Jason told her.

Azalina took her father's hand. "Daddy, he knows what to do. You went away…you went away and everybody died." She was sobbing now, all the grief that was pent up in her began to flood to the surface. "Tell him the truth and let him go."

"It's okay. Don't cry. I won't leave you this time," Jason promised.

But Azalina couldn't hold in her fears. She blurted out, "Anna has the JumpDrive from the laptop. Dad gave it to her. I saw him. Is that what you want? Anna, give it to him so he can go. Please. Give it to him."

Roca turned to Anna. "Do what your sister says, Anna."

"What does it matter, there was nothing to back up."

A change came over Roca. His face twisted up, his forehead furrowed and his temper raged. "Why didn't you tell me?"

"If there was nothing on the laptop…"

He held out his hand. "I'm getting really tired of this

argument. Give it to me. I'm not asking you, I'm ordering you."

"He'll just destroy it," Jason said. "Don't give it to him." Anna didn't know if her father was being rational or not, but he seemed to be more coherent and in charge.

Maybe it was inadvertent, just one of those meaningless moves that someone makes when arguing, but Roca's hand slid up to rest on his MP-5. "I don't have time to stand here arguing. Give me the JumpDrive."

The question in her mind was very simple. If there never had been anything on that laptop, and she had to assume he would have been able to know that, then why would there be something on the JumpDrive?

He could have made a mistake about the laptop and just realized it, but Anna was convinced now her father was right. Everything started to make sense. Why hadn't she seen it before?

Roca had a threatening look and Anna didn't react well to threatening looks. "I'll take care of the JumpDrive," she said. "If it's so valuable, it'll give you incentive to get somebody back here in a hurry."

She now had her hands on her weapon.

"You are making the mistake of your life," Roca said.

The blood seemed to drain from Roca's face. They were standing about ten feet apart.

He's going to do something, she thought.

And for a moment Anna wasn't sure what to do, or how to handle it. Maybe she should just give the damn thing to him!

"Anna, you are interfering with a government agent in the line of duty. You are on the verge of a tragic mistake."

Jason started to tell her what to do, but she told her father to shut up. She couldn't afford any distractions.

Azalina protested. "Give it to him!"

"Let's everybody just settle down. I want to know what's going on," Anna said.

"It's not yours to question," Roca snapped.

"Now it is," she shot back. "I didn't trust anything my father was telling me. Maybe he was right."

Anna had a hard time believing that Roca was actually pointing his gun at her, and with a look in his eyes that told her he'd just as soon shoot her than continue the conversation.

She remembered how easily he'd shot those men in that encampment. The empty look in his eyes, as if nothing out of the ordinary had happened.

And she remembered her father telling her, in his delirium, that Roca had no intention of letting them out of there. She'd found that notion ridiculous at the time, but not now. The dark side of Tom Roca stood before her.

Azalina was crying.

Jason was yelling.

And then she saw Roca do something that really frightened her. His gaze darted to Azalina, then Jason, as if measuring them, trying to determine what order would be most advantageous to his cause.

He would kill them all—just like her father had said he would.

And that's when the part of her that Brock had trained

so intensely with his videos, his thousands of bullets, all his conditioning exercises, came into play.

Azalina started to run and Roca turned his weapon in her direction. Anna swung her own MP-5 around in a short arc and shot Roca in the chest with a 3-round burst.

He dropped to the ground.

The silence was palpable.

The one thing that Brock had said was the hardest for a person to do, she'd done without flinching, without really thinking.

And now she was looking at a man whose life she had taken.

Taken to save her family.

Chapter 24

Anna turned to find Azalina, but she was gone. "Azalina!" Panic swept over her. Had she been hit by a stray bullet? The thought sickened her.

But then, peeking out from behind a tree, the sweet face of her little sister appeared, tears streaking her delicate cheeks, and eyes showing all the anguish of mind-numbing fear.

Jason yelled at her to come to him and she did, ignoring Roca lying on the ground, her face all twisted in confusion and misery. When she got to her father, she hung on tight. Jason sat on a fallen tree and held her for a long time.

"He was going to hurt you," Jason said. "Anna had

no choice but to stop him. He was a very bad man who tricked you into thinking he was a good man."

Anna had no time for angst. She knew the jihad soldiers would be on them at any minute.

"We have to go. Now! Azalina, I want you to go up first. You know the way. You're a big brave girl, and we need you to be our guide out of here. Now hurry. I'll help Dad. When you get to the top, watch for the soldiers. Go!"

A sense of desperation hit Anna hard. She felt trapped and she didn't like the feeling. Her mind went back to when she was in high school watching the Storm King Mountain fire her father was fighting. That moment when she learned that the burn-over had trapped and killed an unknown number of firefighters. She remembered the desperate feeling of rushing home to her mother, hoping against hope that her father was all right.

It was a long, cruel wait before she learned that her dad wasn't one of the fourteen firefighters who died that day. She'd had nightmares for a year afterward. It was then she decided to become, like her father, a smoke jumper. He had been responsible for saving so many other lives. She wanted to do the same.

Maybe part of the reason was knowing her father was a risk taker and that her being with him during fire seasons would cut down that adventurous side of him. Little did she realize that she would become a high-risk taker herself.

Now, helping him move off the mountain, she understood they were finally, as he always put it when she was little, dancing with fire.

Together.

"Hand me Roca's gun," Jason said.

Anna stripped the weapon off Roca's body and handed it to her dad. Then she removed Roca's pack containing his Sat radio and added it to her own gear. In the meantime, Azalina found a clear opening up the bank.

Next, she tossed the walking sticks, one by one, up to Azalina. She caught them with no problem.

"You have quite an arm," Jason told her.

"I pitched a little softball," Anna answered.

"That's right, you did. I'd forgotten all about that. You always were impressive in whatever sport you tried."

"Good parents make good coaches," she said with a wink.

Anna decided the best way was for her to act as an anchor for his wounded leg. He still had strong arms and hands and could grab the roots and pull himself up using his one good leg, then she would curl her arm under the wounded leg and hoist it up.

Then move herself up.

And do it all over again.

Using this method, they scaled the steep incline. Once on top, Jason insisted on carrying Roca's pack.

They found themselves on new terrain now. Patchy lava rocks, heavy with bush and short trees.

Anna took her father's left arm around her shoulder and got a grip on his left wrist with her hand, her right arm around his waist. He could walk as long as she was supporting much of his weight. It left her MP-5 suspended across her chest.

They'd gone about fifty yards when Azalina spotted the jihad soldiers coming right toward them. Anna saw them a split second before they saw her.

Four of them.

All wearing face masks against the smoke. All carrying automatic rifles.

It was a short, intense firefight. She instinctively went for the two men who veered to the left, and her father took the one who veered to the right. Azalina lay on the ground behind Anna and her father, never saying a word.

The lead man went down like a rug had been pulled out from under him. The man behind him tried to get his weapon into play, but she hit him with a second burst. Her father took down the other two.

She glanced at her father. His face was screwed up in pain, his body being pushed forward by sheer will-power. Even wounded and sick he had that Quick refusal to quit, to surrender. He would go until he dropped.

Then he'd crawl.

Azalina wanted to help him, but he refused, insisting he was okay. From then on they kept Azalina between them to protect her from any further gunfire. When Anna looked at her, she wore a stoic, expressionless face. Anna could only hope that all of this would someday fade into Azalina's past.

They walked on for a bit more until a noise came rushing up from the valley below. A roar that she recognized.

A fire blowup. A tidal wave of fire that would consume everything in its path.

Jason, more alive now than at any time she'd seen before, obviously recognized the sound. He picked up his speed, moving with just one of the bamboo sticks, the other arm occupied with the submachine gun. He hobbled, but he hobbled fast, giving Anna a knowing look.

Anna used the Sat phone and spoke to Brock, telling him a chopper could reach them where they were.

"How far away are you? The fire is closing in," Anna said. The smoke was so thick she could hardly talk without coughing.

"Five minutes. Where's Roca?" Brock asked. "We haven't been able to contact him."

"He's dead," she said without hesitation.

There was a moment of silence on her phone. Then, "Copy that" was all he said.

Bethesda, Maryland

Stanford Ellis got the message from his source at CIA headquarters at one o'clock in the afternoon. It was sent on a one-time pad, the oldest and still the safest form of cryptography.

An hour later, as he waited along the jogging trail that looped down to the Potomac, he watched the gulls gliding about on the tidal air in gentle swooping motions.

He allowed himself a cigarette. He took short puffs, but inhaled deeply and held on to the smoke as if trying to leech out every droplet of nicotine, before releasing it in a long exhale. He limited himself to four or five a day. His health wasn't good anyway, so the bad effect on his lungs or heart didn't worry him much. Life was short, but one's actions were long in consequences. His would be historic.

Operation Blowback was in the critical stage now. Timing was everything. Timing and a little luck.

Ellis watched his former protégé at the CIA come toward him.

"He get it yet?" Ellis asked as the jogger slowed to a walk and came over to him.

"No word yet. But they've found Quick in a cave up on the side of a mountain. He's in bad shape," Frank Patterson said.

"Makes it easier."

"What about Anna Quick?"

"Bringing her out might not be a good idea if she's had any chance to talk to her father. No, she can't come out."

"The guide that took them in turns out to be a ten-year-old girl. Speaks fluent English."

"Who the hell is she?" Ellis took another drag on his cigarette, but didn't bother to keep the smoke in this time.

"Don't know. I'm trying to find out."

"That's too bad. Nobody comes out but Roca."

"That's what I ordered."

When he was alone again, Ellis decided he'd wasted the first cigarette and so it didn't count.

He lit another and sucked in the smoke greedily as he imagined the cargo ship that was en route to Marseilles and how close it might be.

He knew of six other cargo carriers that had left Jacarta in the timeframe that Jason Quick had warned them about. His carrier was a fast, 11,000-ton monohull with a thousand containers.

That ship, flagged Liberian, would be only a day from the French coastline, then switch to another ship before heading to the States.

Ellis knew now they would stop Jason Quick. He felt safe. The cargo would reach its final destination and the world would change forever.

There is a God, he thought, smiling to himself.

The talking heads on the panel TV shows who thought the war was winding down would soon learn what fools they were. This war was still in its early rounds. Still in the feeling-out stage.

The Islamists wanted a war with the West. Well, they were going to get their wish. But this wouldn't look like Vietnam. This was going to look a lot more like World War III, once Ellis was back in charge.

Part Five
Operation Blowback

Chapter 25

Pouco Vulcao Island

The lava field opened in the jungle like a wound.

Anna, Jason and Azalina crawled into the opening, making their way over the black rocks and keeping as low as possible to escape the gunfire that was now crackling from the distant treeline.

When Anna found a crevice that would contain them and give her a field of fire, she stopped.

"Dad, stay down. Azalina, lie right next to him," she ordered.

Anna felt the heat pressing on her from the lava rock and from the superheated air above her. Her skin pulled tight against her face as if it was shrinking under the assault.

Bullets hit the rocks around them and careened off with a shrill whine. This lava rock pile had to be the hottest spot on the island, building heat throughout the day with nowhere to escape at night because of the surrounding fires. The winds were dry, and vacillated, reminding her of the nasty Santa Anas that blew down out of the deserts into the funnels of the California landscape, turning small fires into blazing hurricanes.

The sky overhead glowed a molten red, reflecting the fires that were now completely out of control. The roar of the burning trees and brush was punctuated by the crackle of automatic weapons as the guerrilla fighters advanced across the lava rocks toward their hiding place, pinning them in their narrow and shallow crevice.

This, Anna thought, is what hell must feel like.

Azalina lay between them in the fetal position, softly whimpering. Jason was lying on his back, trying to calm her, assure her they weren't going to die. He held Roca's MP-5 in his hands.

Anna crawled to a position where she could see the approaching fighters bathed in the fire's glow. They moved from one rock formation to another, covering each other's approaches with bursts from their weapons. She could no longer hold back. Up until now, she'd done so in order to keep them from locating her exact position, but now they were getting too close. She fired three short bursts at the dark figures, then sank away from the incoming return gunfire.

Brock's welcome voice came through over her headset. "Anna, you read?"

"Yes. Loud and clear." Never had she been so happy to hear a voice in all her life.

"We're coming in. What is your situation?"

"Not good. We're in a crevice. We're taking gunfire." Another round burst over her head, causing her to sink lower, scratching her hands and arms on the porous rocks.

"How many hostile forces?"

"I don't know. A dozen, maybe more."

"Do you have the flare gun?"

"Yes."

"In five minutes, put one up. Copy?"

"Yes. That's a date." Five minutes would be an eternity. She wanted him to be there right now.

"And keep your head down."

"Count on it."

Anna took the flare gun out of her pack, loaded and cocked the gun, then waited.

Her father crawled up beside her. "You okay?"

"The choppers are five minutes away."

Anna and her father could hear the guerrilla fighters talking on their radios. She didn't understand what they were saying, but her father did.

He listened for a minute, completely focused on their chatter. "They're preparing an assault. How many pellets do you have for the flare gun?"

"Three."

"Good. Use one. Maybe it'll scare them into staying put. How many clips do you have?"

"Six."

They had taken four clips from Roca, and Jason still had one seated in the MP-5.

She was relieved to see her father focused and coherent. Especially now, when she needed him most. His fever apparently had broken in the past hour, and he was almost the man she remembered.

Anna fired the flare gun. Moments later the flare blossomed into a cloud of brilliant white light, revealing three groups of men sneaking forward on the rocks. The light startled them just as her dad had thought, and they dropped out of sight.

One man stayed out in the open not more than mere yards from them, with the proverbial deer-in-the-headlights look. Anna felt the counter-tug of resistance even as she fired. Her father fired as well and the man fell forward, facedown on the ground. No one else seemed to move.

She could breathe for the moment.

Brock sat in the open door of the lead chopper. They raced in like dark birds of prey, skimming fifteen feet above the roiling chop of the sea. In the distance he now could make out the island squatting beneath its smoke plumes.

A white light flashed like a bolt of lightning deep in the clouds. She'd fired the flare early. Something was happening.

Brock felt the desperate frustration of wanting to go faster, get there sooner, but knowing he couldn't. No feeling was worse than realizing somebody needed help and not being able to get to them.

He picked up his Sat radio. "Anna, you read?"

But she didn't answer. He waited a moment, trying to remain calm and trust her strength. "Anna, are you there?"

"Yes." He relaxed his grip on the radio.

"What's happening? You fired a flare too early." Brock had her coordinates from both hers and Jason's transponders, but with the choppers moving so fast he wanted a visual to pinpoint their exact location. Plus, he wanted to actually see where the choppers could land.

"We needed to stop their advance. I have two more."

"We're only a couple minutes out. Let one go now."

"Will do."

The minutes seemed like hours, but finally the choppers were racing over burning canopy. Brock felt the heat blast on his face. He pulled his legs in now as they skirted the treetops and headed for the blossom of white light that gave them the exact location.

Anna felt the change. She didn't realize why for a moment or two. But she sensed something in the movement, in the attitude of the battlefield.

Then she understood. A sound that was beautiful, sweet and glorious. Like nothing else the entire world.

A symphony both familiar and yet never appreciated so much as now. The *whap whap whap* of choppers as they charged into the battlefield, like giant friendly dragons swooping down from the sky, breathing fire on her enemies.

No Fourth of July fireworks celebration could compare in beauty to the fireworks coming from those choppers, the piston-like rage of the cannons, the *rat-a-tat-tat* of the machine guns and the *whoosh* and *boom* of the rockets as they snaked down to the ground to impact on the guerrilla positions and returning gunfire in great bursts of power.

In her mind she cheered every violent blast, every thunderous explosion.

Anna became aware of all of it now. Shadow and light. Sounds. The choppers. The fire raging around them. Men crashing around in the jungle. Bullets slamming into the night. Everything happening at once.

She was also aware of what she'd done and how it had happened without thought, without reservation. Now aware of her mind and her body, she got ready to move with deliberate speed and caution toward the landing zone.

She was in awe of the ferocity of the gunfire from the choppers as they circled. And the anger of the return fire.

Now she understood. This was a soldier's world. Mad, violent chaos. This was the nature of combat.

It had opened up a part of her she didn't know existed. Everything in her was focused on their escape, ready to kill anything that got in her path. She was determined to get herself and her family out alive, and nothing else mattered.

C'mon, c'mon, she urged silently as one of the Pave Low choppers attempted a landing.

She turned to Jason, who now held Azalina close to him. "Get ready to run."

"I'm scared," Azalina blurted out.

Anna bent down. "Don't be. I promise, nothing is going to hurt us. We're going to get out of this. All three of us. You have my word."

They all hugged for a moment. Then Anna stood up and put her focus back on the task at hand.

The second chopper swung in close over the battlefield now, laying down a withering barrage of cannon fire, driving the guerrilla fighters back.

Anna had a moment of panic when she thought the lead chopper was going to crash, the way it swung wildly as it descended. In the last hundred feet it dropped like a rock, then stopped in a hover about twenty feet off the ground with its sister ship right behind.

The door gunner beside Brock began a steady drumbeat of return fire, hammering the guerrilla fighters on the perimeters.

The chopper slanted across the tops of the trees. In the open door of the chopper, Brock scanned the lava field below with his night-vision binoculars.

A bullet hit the door gunner in the shoulder and he fell back. Brock made sure the wound wasn't fatal, while DeAngelo replaced the gunner.

Brock returned to the open doorway and searched for targets as more rounds smacked into the chopper. He could hear over his headset that the second helicopter was also taking hits.

Somebody else in the chopper yelled that he'd been hit. "Bring it in! Bring it in!" Brock yelled over his headset. They had to get down fast and get out fast.

The chopper shuddered, lurched and the pilot had to fight to bring it under control.

Brock felt the heat of a bullet zing pass his ear. He returned fire at the origin of every tracer round that he could see coming at him.

Brock searched for Anna, Jason and the girl. He spotted them as they came out into the open, but they were under heavy fire. Both Jason and Anna were firing back.

"Anna, go, go, go!" Brock yelled. "Bring it down. Now!" he ordered the pilot.

Brock's mind went into a different mode when he flew in over a battlefield. Sometimes, and now was one of them, he stopped hearing the sounds of battle. Things just went silent in his head. And movement slowed down. It was like a scene from a Kurosawa movie where everything was in slow motion with no sound whatsoever.

Just a visual.

Just the war.

Brock glanced around at his men and gave the signal. These were his team and together they'd gone on dozens of missions all over the world. He knew their habits and they knew his. They could go for days with virtually no conversation outside of tactical gestures. They were so well trained and so conditioned by the number of missions they'd done, that the routines were becoming automatic. Each man understood what he had to do. They worked out the mission details endlessly to simplify every move.

As the chopper dropped toward the ground, DeAngelo threw out the fast ropes. Brock pulled on his gloves for the descent, Swartzlander moved in right behind him. Another door gunner continued with relentless dispassion to lay down cover fire as the second chopper circled with its cannons blazing.

Brock stared into the glow of the furnace in search of Anna Quick and her family.

"She's the exception to the rule," Swartzlander offered. He wasn't one to back off his opinion about anything. He just made exceptions. That way he could continue to believe what he wanted in the face of contrary evidence.

"And then some," Brock added. "Let's go."

The pilot banked hard and hovered. Tracer bullets raced up to greet them.

Chapter 26

Anna grabbed Azalina's hand. "Stay with me. Dad, let's go. Dad—"

But he wasn't moving.

"You two go," he said. "I'll stay and cover you."

"No. I didn't do all this to leave you here. You're coming with us, or none of us leave."

She stared at him, never flinching. Never wavering in her resolve.

"Anna, we may not make it if we all go out for that helicopter. It's too much of a risk."

"Dad, we're nothing if we're not risktakers."

"Daddy, you promised me. I won't leave you here." Azalina grabbed her father's arm and held on.

"You promised us both. Now let's get off this damn island before one of us gets shot," Anna said.

Jason gazed down at Azalina. "You're right. I promised." He took in a deep breath and released it slowly. "Let's go."

Anna grabbed his other arm and the three of them headed for the chopper.

"Go, go, go!" Brock screamed.

Three men dropped out of the chopper, sliding down the ropes so fast they were on the ground before Brock could catch his breath.

DeAngelo and Swartzlander instantly laid down cover fire as Brock sprinted toward Anna and her family.

Jason's leg gave out and he stumbled. Brock reached him in time, grabbed him, turned and pulled him up in a fireman's carry and headed for the chopper. Azalina and Anna ran in tight to Brock's side.

The pilot settled as Brock pushed everyone up, one after another and then climbed in as the helicopter took off.

As they raced up over the canopy, Anna caught a glimpse of the second chopper pulling up and out behind them. It seemed like a miracle that they'd all made it out alive.

Brock sat down beside Anna.

"I've had bad dates before, Quick," Brock yelled over the roar of the fire below and the whine of the rotors, "but this is ridiculous."

"Sorry about that," she yelled back. "I'll try for dinner and a movie next time."

"I'm going to hold you to that."

"I hope you do."

He smiled at her, and she wanted to simply melt into his arms, but it was then that she noticed that the two men who had helped rescue them, DeAngelo and Swartzlander, were both wounded. They were sitting across from her trying to deal with their injuries. A third man administered first aid.

Pieces of the chopper had been shot off and there was debris everywhere she looked. She was amazed the thing could fly.

As she turned to see how Azalina and her father were doing, the chopper sputtered, coughed but then regained its regular hum.

Jason sat next to Azalina while she rested her head on his chest. He soothed his child, running his hand over her hair and whispering that they were safe now. It gave Anna a warm feeling to see the two of them together, but it also reminded her of what the real mission was all about. Saving lives.

Anna extracted the thumb-size JumpDrive from her pocket and handed it to Brock. "Everything that was on the laptop should be on there," she said, her voice filling with emotion.

Brock took the JumpDrive, running his fingers over it as he glanced at her, looking confused.

"I thought the laptop was empty."

"I don't think it was."

"But Roca said—"

"He lied."

"It's imperative," Jason shouted, "that we get that code broken and the information out as soon as possible."

Brock turned to Jason, saying, "He had headquarters believing that you fabricated the whole terrorist crisis just to get your daughter—" Brock glanced at Azalina "—out."

"That was some of it, I admit, but the threat is real and we're running on borrowed time now. You need to break that code as soon as we land and act on the information. It's imperative that you don't let Curtis Verrill anywhere near that information."

"I understand," Brock said, and slipped the memory stick into a secure pocket on his jumpsuit.

Anna stared out the chopper's open door at the dark waters of the Strait of Malacca one hundred feet below. The last day or so seemed like a nightmare that she was finally going to awaken from. She wanted to tell Brock the truth about Roca, so there would be no confusion later.

"Roca destroyed the laptop," she told him. "Then when he found out about the JumpDrive, he tried to take it by force. I had no choice. I shot him."

Brock's eyes widened.

"My father was never supposed to leave that island," Anna said. "Actually, Roca intended to be the only one coming out. He was going to leave all of us there, or kill us. Either way, it didn't seem to matter to him as long as we didn't come out with him. I had to—"

There was an intense shudder in one of the engines, followed by sudden and violent shaking. This time it didn't stop. There was a sound of grinding metal. The engine coughed and choked and everybody knew they were in trouble.

"How far away is the ship?" Anna yelled over the shattering noise.

"About thirty minutes," Brock yelled back as he pulled an inflatable dinghy out from under one of the seats. Then he pulled life jackets down off hooks and began tossing them to everyone.

Anna heard the pilot talking to the trailing chopper, informing him of their crisis, then he turned back to everyone and yelled, "We're going down. Hang on. It's gonna be a rough landing."

Chapter 27

Anna helped Azalina on with her life jacket, then slipped her own on when the chopper twisted violently. It didn't spin at first, just lost power and dropped, then gyrated left, then right. Everyone held on to something. Incredibly, no one panicked. No one screamed, not even Azalina. It was just something that was happening to them and they all seemed prepared for whatever their fate would be.

They plunged into the dark sea, hitting the water with a crunching thud. The rotors threw the chopper over on its side, causing everyone to tumble over and over. The sound of twisting metal hitting water was ear shattering.

Then they were sinking.

Anna tried to pull Azalina along with her, but she wouldn't let go of Jason. She was screaming for her father in Malay.

Anna yelled that he would be okay, and to come with her, but Azalina held on tight. Brock grabbed Azalina and tore her away from Jason.

Anna grabbed the door frame for support, reached over and grabbed her father's outstretched arm as he pulled himself up over the lip of the door. She dragged him out into the open water, away from the sinking helicopter.

Brock and DeAngelo, in spite of his wounds, were pulling the other men out. In the darkness there was a calm efficiency about getting everyone out of the rapidly sinking chopper.

Someone had managed to get the dinghy inflated, and Anna helped Jason up into it. Azalina was already inside along with DeAngelo. Brock, Anna, the pilot and the rest of the team remained in the water, holding on to the sides of the small rubber boat, trying to stay together.

The other chopper had circled back and beamed a powerful light down on the crash sight. Anna knew that the Pave Low was one of the top rescue birds in the air force. The pilot already had it moving into position to hoist everyone up from the cold rough sea.

Anna turned and saw Swartzlander a few feet away, struggling to stay above water. Apparently, he'd never gotten into his life jacket. Without hesitation, she swam out for him, took hold of him under his arms and worked herself slowly back to the dinghy as the choppy water tried to push them in the opposite direction.

The massive bulk of their helicopter finally sank out of sight like some great wounded beast.

In the midst of the rescue efforts, two gunboats appeared from behind one of the small nearby clusters of islands and began firing at them with machine guns and shoulder rockets.

Will it never end? Anna thought.

The rescue chopper was forced to pull out and begin defensive maneuvers, leaving everyone behind. The Pave machine gun rounds ripped into one of the boats and it exploded into a fireball, bringing a wild cheer from everyone in the water.

The second boat, apparently realizing it would soon come to the same end, made a dash for the islands, but the chopper easily tracked it down and destroyed it. Then it circled around and came back.

It took about twenty-five minutes to get everyone hoisted up and on board. Anna and Swartzlander were the last two, and a medic instantly tended to Swartzlander.

Brock gave Anna a blanket and she and Azalina huddled together, trying to get their shaking to stop.

Twenty minutes later the helicopter settled down on the deck of the *Hammond*.

The wounded were taken to sick bay for immediate medical attention, and that included Jason—with Azalina not letting him out of her sight—along with DeAngelo and Swartzlander.

Brock and Anna headed for the communications

room to check out the JumpDrive. On the way, Anna chided herself for worrying about her fate if the memory stick was empty. Then she got angry at herself for doubting her father. She dismissed her tangled emotions and decided to focus on what was, rather than what might be.

When they got into the communications area, she was amazed by the enormity of it. It took up half of the ship and housed every piece of sophisticated high-tech gear imaginable.

Brock sat in front of a sleek black monitor and pulled the JumpDrive out of his waterproof pocket.

Verrill intercepted before he could slip it into the USB port.

"Brock, what's that?" Verrill snapped.

Anna held her breath.

Brock wasn't in the mood to deal with Verrill now, but he knew he had no choice. He was attached to the unit under Verrill's direction. Technically, Verrill was not only his superior, but his commander within the scope of the operation. But at the same time, Special Ops was under the ultimate direction of SOCOM. He didn't have time to get into a tug-of-war over the jurisdiction of the memory stick.

"I have possession of the device and I'm going to make sure it gets properly loaded and reviewed."

"Where's Roca?"

"He didn't make it out."

"His body still on the island?"

"Yes."

Verrill glanced at Anna. "How did Roca die?" he asked with an accusing voice.

Brock answered for her. "We have no time for a debriefing. It'll have to wait."

Verrill's face turned red. "You better hand over that JumpDrive, soldier, or you're risking serious consequences. I'll have you arrested on the spot. You want to end up in Leavenworth?"

In his peripheral vision, Brock saw every face in the room turn toward them. No one spoke. Beyond the hum of computers and a few printers, there wasn't a sound.

This was exactly the kind of situation Brock never wanted to face. The idea of defying a superior officer, even from the CIA, was basically unthinkable. Yet he knew that was exactly what he had to do.

Brock stood to face Verrill. "I'm maintaining control of this device and everything that's on it. I will be the one to determine what to do with its contents."

"The hell you will!"

"And I'm going to have to ask you to go to quarters and remain there until we dock."

"Who the hell—" Verrill turned to give orders to the men and women in the room but Brock did the unthinkable, he put his gun in Verrill's face.

"This *blended* operation is now separated. I'm operating under Title Ten and you are operating under Title Fifty. Consider it a divorce with prejudice. Get the hell out of here."

The collection of highly trained men and women in

the room, specialists from every branch of the service, were witnesses to something that would either lead to Brock's downfall, or Verrill's. At the moment Brock was banking on the latter.

Brock turned to two officers, one a Navy SEAL, and the other a woman from Air Rescue. "See that this man is not allowed back in this room and that he doesn't have the run of the ship. And make sure he has no means of communication on him."

"You listen to this maniac, your careers will be over."

Verrill broke into something of a tirade before they got him out of there.

Brock sat back down and inserted the JumpDrive into the USB port. "Let's just hope that your father is the man we both think he is."

When the window came up, he clicked on Open but a message came up saying that he was an illegal user. He pulled out the device and went over to one of the computers they used to break encryption and inserted it into the USB port and waited. Anna paced behind him.

The first shout came when the drive proved to have several files rather than empty space.

"Well, we've got something," Brock said. "Now let's see if we can read it." He pulled up a code-breaking program and went to work.

Anna watched as Brock maneuvered programs and files at lightning speed. He told her that he was searching for signs of viruses built in to corrupt the files in the event of an attempted entry. When he found one, he set off a program to destroy it. He talked the whole time like he was playing some video game. Every time something happened that he liked, he would ask rhetorically, "Am I good, or what? You can run but you can't hide."

Anna couldn't help but laugh.

This went on for about an hour. Several other men and women began to watch as Brock played with the data. Every minor victory brought a round of applause. Anna felt a sigh of relief. They had a lot more files to go through, but he was in and the files were intact.

The next program he ran had to do with encryption and then translation. He said that would take a good twenty minutes. "If you'd like to get into some dry clothes, one of the navy seamen will show you where to clean up and change."

She accepted the offer with gratitude. She'd had two really bad days and wanted nothing more than to get out of her damp clothes and into something a little less army.

Anna stopped in sick bay to check on her father and Azalina. She told her dad about the confrontation with Verrill.

"Good," Jason said, looking much better now that he was cleaned up, shaven and smiling.

Anna still had a few doubts about that JumpDrive. "You haven't seen it yourself. Maybe what you expected to be there isn't."

"The man I took it from died to protect it. I think it's the real thing. Don't worry, Verrill and Roca wouldn't have launched this operation if they didn't know for a fact there was information they didn't want getting out on that computer."

Anna then admitted, "Roca had me. When he started treating Azalina decently, I started thinking he was a great guy."

"Maybe he was, with kids. Some of the worst men who ever lived were great with kids. Besides, fooling people was his profession," Jason said. "He was always well versed at tactical lying and deception."

"Will there be an investigation? Shooting a CIA agent—"

"Let Brock handle it after he gets all the information. If it becomes an issue, we'll deal with it. Depends on how this all shakes out. For right now, Roca died on a mission in defense of his country. For your part, you were never here. Never saw any island and know nothing. That's how it'll be played. You never heard of the Strait of Malacca."

Anna sat with Azalina for a few minutes. She seemed, at least on the surface, to still be handling it all very well.

Anna could hardly imagine the depth of her sister's strength that allowed her to endure everything that she'd gone through. It was beyond amazing. Only time would tell how much of an impact it was going to have on her later. No one completely escaped without some post-traumatic symptoms. What mattered was that they had plenty of love and help dealing with it when it hit.

Anna went back out into the passageway and the navy

seaman Brock directed to help her out, a straitlaced-looking girl who looked about eighteen, escorted her to the captain's quarters where she could shower and get changed. She asked Anna what size she needed, and disappeared, leaving Anna with a bar of soap, a clean white towel, a regulation black comb, a small bottle of some nameless shampoo and really unattractive underwear.

If nothing else, at least the towel was soft.

Chapter 28

When Anna returned to the communications room in a clean set of fatigues she felt renewed.

The moment she walked in she felt the tension. Everyone was quiet. Four men were at the console where she'd left Brock. He was on the phone.

Something was going on, something big. The ship's captain and officers were standing behind Brock.

Anna felt the tension grow in her gut.

Brock got off the phone. He turned and saw her there. He left the room and motioned her to follow him. They went up on deck.

"What's going on?" Anna asked. "Did you get anything?"

He leaned back against the railing and nodded. "You want to take a trip?"

"Where?"

"The Mediterranean. Somewhere between Malta and Tunisia."

She was elated and shocked at the same time. "You found the ship?"

"We found the ship."

"Then he wasn't out of his mind."

"Your father may have been sick with fever, but he wasn't delusional. He was exactly right. We just found the most indepth operational database we've ever come across."

"Where's the ship headed?"

"Marseilles. But it looks like Washington, D.C. is the final destination for the bad stuff."

"The bad stuff?"

"Enough uranium to make a couple of very dirty bombs."

"Does Dad know?"

"Yes. I told him about ten minutes ago."

"And Verrill?"

"He knows. And he knows he's in trouble."

"What kind of trouble?"

"Big trouble. There were code names in that file of people who were indirectly and directly involved in keeping this ship's cargo and destination a big secret. People who were, in effect, preventing any warnings about it from getting out. People who were, in essence, protecting it. And the people behind the plot to deliver the material knew who these men were and had code names for them."

"Americans."

Brock nodded. "A little cabal of disgruntled intelligence operatives working, it appears, for the man who once ran all intelligence operations in this area of the world. We don't know the motive yet, but we'll get it."

"Then all those crazy ramblings of my father when he was in the midst of his fever delirium are, in fact, true."

"Yes."

"They stop the ship?"

"Not yet. They're tracking it. Since we're the ones with the container identities, I thought it fitting that we should be there. If, that is, you feel like traveling."

"Traveling with you is risky business."

"But fun," he said, winking at her.

Anna laughed. "In a perverse sort of way. When do we leave?"

"About twenty minutes."

"So, we don't know if, in fact, this uranium is really there."

"We think it is. But no, we don't know until we go there, interdict the ship, find the containers and bombard them with a neutron gun that can detect through the lead casing."

"What kind of ship is it?"

"It's a thirty-thousand-ton container, Liberian flagged. Left Jakarta four days ago. Made two stops and the next one is where we can catch them. If we miss it in Marseilles, we have no idea how it's getting to D.C. This is out best shot."

"What if the uranium isn't there?"

"Well," he said, "that would mean we're all victims of the most elaborate and meaningless and complex hoax ever created—or the minute the laptop went missing it was off-loaded ship to ship and is headed to some other port. Then we're screwed. I like to think that didn't happen, that they didn't have time to make new arrangements." He paused, then, "You know, you'd make a very good operational planner."

"Why is that?"

"You never let a negative scenario get past you."

"Smoke-jumping habit. Negative scenarios are the only ones that concern us. It's the business of what can go wrong."

"Like I said, you'd make a great planner. That's also our business."

"So, what are the travel arrangements?"

"We'll take the Pav Low, hop four hundred miles to the nearest carrier, jet to the Mediterranean Sea and land on the USS *Ronald Reagan.* The interdiction will be handled from there. I didn't know if you wanted to be on the inital assault team—"

"Are you asking? Because if you're asking, don't bother. Why go at all if I can't be in on the finish."

"Yeah, I assumed as much. I laid my career on the line by putting that demand in with SOCOM. They've agreed, but without officially signing on."

"I am, therefore I don't exist."

"For the boys on top. That's the beauty of operational deniability. They can't fail. A failed operation never happened."

"The ultimate in covering your ass."

"Yeah. Your father and Azalina will be heading to the States not long after we leave. If you want to go say goodbye, do it now. This bus is leaving in—" he glanced at his watch "—thirteen minutes. Not that I need to remind you—"

"I heard nothing, know nothing," she finished for him. "Is everything always such a rush with you guys?"

"We can be slow...when we need to be," he said with a sexy smile.

Anna started to blush. *That smile gets me every time,* she thought. "I'll believe it when I see it."

"Stick around. Once this little mission is over, there should be some downtime."

"Are you flirting with me?"

"In my own humble way."

"You, humble? Yeah, right. Save me a seat, I'll be right back."

Brock watched her walk away. There were walks and then there were walks. She had something special going on, no doubt. Part of it was her being tall and an athlete. But most of it was just plain ballsy attitude. The roll was not just in the hips, it was in the shoulders. And she didn't just walk so much as she strode. It was a great mix of cocky fighter, cool street smarts and beautiful, sexy woman. Brock wanted to follow her around all day long just to watch that walk.

This lady is going to be big trouble for me, Brock thought. Big trouble.

Bethesda, Maryland

Stanford Ellis picked up the phone on his secure line.

"There's a problem," Frank Patterson said.

"What kind of problem?"

"We're monitoring the ship's communications and there's chaos. And something about one of those little JumpDrives. A backup."

Ellis didn't like the sound of that. "We get it?"

"Don't know yet."

"What do you mean?"

"Verrill's got some problems on board the freighter with the goddamn Special Operations. They've more or less taken over the ship."

"How do you *more or less take over the ship?* That's mutiny."

"That's how it looks."

Stanford Ellis had been walking Liddy, his beloved Great Dane. He'd been admiring the lawns of his estate when he'd gotten the call that he thought would be good news, not looming disaster.

"I don't understand how Verrill could let this happen," Ellis said bitterly.

"He's lost control of the situation and he can't go up the chain of command to do anything about it. You know that. And it's not technically a mutiny. What they have done is get cooperation from the ship's commander."

"What about Roca?"

"Apparently he's dead," Patterson replied.

"Apparently? Do we know anything for sure?"

"No."

"You listen to me. I don't care what Verrill has to do, he's got to take back control of that freighter and the situation. It's a Black Operation. It can be buried no matter what happens, so do something. Do it now. If you don't find a way to stop this…"

He didn't have to finish. He hung up and put the phone back in his pocket. Damn Jason Quick, he thought angrily. Ellis had personally recruited, groomed and used Quick in one of the most brilliant operations ever. And Quick had never known the real game. Jason Quick had been a brilliant asset. And he'd inadvertently offered up the opportunity that Ellis and his group were looking for.

It couldn't be lost. Not now. Not when they were so close. Ellis knew the ship was still a half day from port.

Operation Blowback was still alive.

This was all Verrill's fault. It'd been his decision to go after Quick rather than let him rot on that island. It was his fear that the laptop had more on it than just the terrorist mastermind's planned operations. Verrill was afraid there was a list of names.

And what happened to Roca? All he had to do was kill Jason and get out with the laptop. Moron. Couldn't do anything right.

Ellis couldn't stand not knowing what was going on aboard the *Hammond*. If they had a backup, would they be able to break into it in time? And if they did, what would they find?

And if they found the details of the operation, would SOCOM believe them *in time?*

Ellis headed for the house across the vast stretch of his estate, while Liddy was running about chasing birds. One weak link, Ellis thought, and the whole thing is in jeopardy. His stomach was acting up and he needed something to calm it down.

Just a little bit of luck. That's all they needed to change the course of this war—and the course of history—and pay back the traitors in Washington who had booted him out. Just a little luck and a few more hours.

Blowback simply could not fail.

Chapter 29

Mediterranean Sea

This time they had it right. This time, Anna thought as she sat next to Brock as the choppers pulled away from the carrier USS *Ronald Reagan* and headed for the target, the thirty-thousand-ton container ship *Estrela Norte,* she was going in with her mentor.

The roller-coaster ride wasn't yet over. And part of her didn't want it to be over. She knew it was an absurd notion, but the truth was, she liked this. Not just the adrenaline-junkie-excitement of it for her, but the importance, and even more, the idea that for the moment, she was part of this incredible team, about to save thousands of lives.

Brock handed her a pair of leather gloves. "Those fast ropes will burn the skin off your hands."

"We expecting much resistance?"

"Depends on how stealthy we take her. You never know, but there might be. Just another foray into a bad neighborhood."

"Story of your life?"

"Yeah."

The commandos with them were men she had just met. They were donning their Kevlar helmets with night-vision goggles and she did the same. Weapons checked. Radios checked. The ship had been laid out on the screen and divided up for the different teams. Theirs would be hitting the aft deck. One man was designated for the passageway, two each for cabin and compartment entry. The ship would be cleared first of personnel, all to be corralled on deck. Then the search for the containers would begin.

Everyone fell silent now, getting their minds ready. She glanced around at the stoic faces. The guy across from her looked like a young Denzel Washington. Next to him sat a guy they called Kansas. He looked like he was sixteen. Six altogether in this lead team.

The helicopter slid across the soft chop, the water gleaming in the moonlight like bits of bright metal. The container ship moved at about twelve knots and there was no indication they knew what was about to hit them from the air and sea.

Simultaneous with the air assault, Navy SEALs were closing in their swift boats.

Anna tightened her gloves, checked her assault rifle and her thigh-rig.

Green light. Time to go.

She felt a surge of excitement and energy. Brock gave her a thumbs-up.

The helicopter skimmed so low to the waves, well below radar, that she could feel the spray.

The next minute she was sliding down a rope onto the deck and moving into position, her goggles down over her eyes. From that moment on it went like clockwork. Passageways secured. Wheelhouse secured. They hit the cabins, took prisoners, had them escorted to the upper deck and then moved on, cabin to cabin, compartment to compartment.

It took all of about thirty minutes to secure the ship. They had hit so fast and unexpected that there was no resistance.

Brock had already given out the container numbers and now the search was on for them. There were over five hundred containers on deck, and nine hundred below. The great fear Brock had was that this was a decoy and that the real thing was already unloading or unloaded at some other port.

It took ninety minutes to disprove that fear. It came over everyone's earpiece.

"We got it!"

The neutron gun, the only quick way to find plutonium encased in lead, had done its job.

After getting a look at the container, Brock and Anna exchanged high fives, then went up on deck. Brock handed her a satellite phone. "I told your father you'd call the minute we found it. He's got a secure phone."

Anna made the call. "Dad, we found it."

"Hey, that's great, just great. You did a fantastic job, Anna, just fantastic."

"I had good role models growing up. How is Azalina?"

"She's doing fine. Sound asleep at the moment."

"I can't wait to see you. I should be home in a few days."

"I'm sure they're going to try and hang on to you for a little while. Love you."

"Love you, too. And give Azalina my love."

She handed the phone to Brock and he spoke with Jason for a few minutes, talking in a kind of code. Anna then called her mother and told her she'd had to take off, but she'd be home soon and not to worry. "No, Mom, I didn't run off and get married."

After she hung up she let out a chuckle. "Mothers. They never quit, do they?"

"They'd better not," Brock said, "or we're all finished. By the way, they're preparing a steak-and-lobster dinner for us on the *Reagan,* if you're interested."

"You have my number."

It was very strange, this idea that they had stopped a plot that could have killed thousands and right now all she could think about was a really good meal—and spending more time with John Brock.

As they walked across the deck to board the chopper for the ride back to the USS. *Reagan,* she said, "Soldier, can I buy you a drink?"

"Anytime, lady, anytime."

* * *

Back on the USS *Ronald Reagan*, Anna, Brock and his team had their steak-and-lobster dinner at 0530 hours. For Anna, whose circadian rhythms were so out of whack her stomach didn't know or care what time of day it was, the meal was fabulous. She ate enough to kill a horse. There was no ceremony, no awards, but they were afforded some serious congratulations on a job well done. Anna didn't think these guys cared much about ceremony and award shows. They preferred to stay in the shadows.

One thing she couldn't escape. She was female, walking shoulder to shoulder with the last bastion of an all-macho world. And what she noticed was that everywhere they went on that carrier was a respect unlike anything she'd ever experienced before. She was part of the elite. And she liked it.

"You are," Brock said, aware of the impact of her presence, "something of a rock star to these boys. You already have a nickname."

"I'm afraid to ask what it is."

"They're calling you Goddess of War. You hang around here much longer you're going to start getting proposals."

"It would make my mother happy."

"Yeah, but it'd break my heart."

Anna laughed. "Yeah, right. I'm sure you're just pining away, Brock."

"Hey, you never know."

"I'll call my mom right now and say I'm engaged to

a man in the most dangerous profession in the world, the one with the shortest life span. And it doesn't even pay well. She'll be thrilled."

Brock laughed. "I'm not proposing marriage."

"What are you proposing?"

"I'll tell you later. But it's definitely not something you want to be telling your mother about. You ready to travel?"

"Where are we going now?"

"Guam. Debriefing. Then we're going to get down and dirty and just see who has the baddest scars."

"That's your proposal?"

"Yeah. You don't like it?"

"It sounds a little like a fetish to me."

"Don't knock it till you've tried it."

"You're pretty cocky. How do you know I'm all that interested?"

"Tell me you aren't and I swear on my ancestors' graves I'll walk right off the edge of this carrier and offer myself to the sharks."

Anna snorted, then belly laughed.

"God, I love that laugh, Quick. It sounds like it was born in a brothel and nourished at a bar."

"Do you always insult the girls you're trying to score with?"

"Only the ones that I'm *really* interested in."

"You need to brush up on your romance skills."

"Can I practice with you?"

"Absolutely."

Bethesda, Maryland

Stanford Ellis heard the words: *They had code names for everybody involved with Blowback.* But he was no longer listening—until he got word National Intelligence agents were coming for him.

He was still in his office on the second-floor corner of his home, with its grand view. The place where the concept of Operation Blowback had been born over a year ago.

Elllis knew it was over and he knew someway, somehow, they'd gotten all the way to him. Verrill. Had to be Verrill, the fool. It's always the weak link that sinks the ship.

Blowback, the most necessary, most important operation of his life, the salvation of not only his name, but of his country, was dead. And the repercussions would be monstrous. Even if the public never knew, and it wouldn't, the intelligence agencies would.

Jason Quick had somehow survived. Ellis had been brought down by one lowly agent.

Stanford Ellis fought down the acid in his stomach and the bitterness in his soul with a double shot of whiskey, then poured another.

He stared with hollow emptiness out the window of his office, seeing but paying no direct attention to the six cars coming through the gate. When he did focus, he thought, *Wasn't one enough?*

Everybody had to get in on the act. Get their ticket punched. Sons of bitches.

He had no intention of giving them any satisfaction whatsoever. Screw them all!

It was a failure. It was inconceivable to him that Quick's daughter, this damn smoke jumper, had been instrumental in thwarting the entire operation.

He glanced sourly at the grandfather clock on the wall as the seconds ticked away. Final seconds. They were coming up the drive now, three black sedans and three black SUVs. Six goddamn vehicles. What did they expect, a shoot-out? Then he saw the choppers swinging in over the water. He smiled. *Everybody* getting their ticket punched. What next, fighters? How about tanks, gentlemen?

Unbidden thoughts rose in his mind. He remembered the bitterness so long ago of his high-school student council president's election. How he'd lost by seven votes. *Seven votes!*

That had changed the entire course of his life. It soured him on politics, on elections. They were always corrupt, always the products of those best organized, the best liars, the most ruthless people. He'd learned a big lesson on that day. He went to law school and then into government service. Behind the scenes. The real power, he'd always believed, was behind the scenes.

And now, even in that struggle, he'd been beaten.

His gaze moved to the pistol on his desk, and the glass of expensive whiskey beside the gun, golden amber in the late-afternoon light.

Failure was unacceptable.

He shook his head in rueful astonishment. How could it be?

Ellis sat down heavily at his mahogany desk. He drank the whiskey in one shot. They had Verrill somewhere, in some secret location, and by the time they got done with him they'd roll up the whole network quickly and quietly.

But they didn't see the big picture. They *thought* they did, but they were afraid to really carry it to its logical conclusion. Even the hawks were cowards.

He reached for the .38-caliber revolver. Such a solid, elegant piece of machinery. A work of art. From caves and clubs to mansions and instruments of elegant design and power. There was poetry in there somewhere.

Ellis, in truth, did considered himself something of a poet as well as writer, warrior, generalist. A Renaissance warrior. Maybe the last of the breed.

He smiled bitterly, knowing now the weak men would win and their victory would give the terrorists the breathing space they needed. He had used them, and once he'd regained his power, was prepared to destroy them. But America's ascendancy to its proper role as not just leader, but as necessary master of the world's destiny, would now not be.

His quest for power was over.

It was a crushing, horrifying, unacceptable notion to Ellis. Totally unacceptable that he had lost this great opportunity for his nation.

He felt the heft of the revolver in his hands.

The single shot resonated with a metallic crispness and sharp finality.

Chapter 30

Guam

Anna sat back in the Humvee and shook her head. "Brock, I can't believe you're taking me out into the damn jungle again. And on our first date."

He chuckled. "You'll like this little spot. It's got ambience."

"Jungle ambience I can do without."

He laughed.

She held on as the Humvee tore into what she thought was a purely imaginary road. She was still fuming about the after-action debriefing that was more like a third-degree interrogation.

"Jeez, Brock, you'd think, instead of saving a good part of the world from misery, we'd committed some kind of crime."

"It's just the way they do things. The beginning of a long process of CIA activities."

It was almost twelve hours of seemingly endless interrogations, or, as they liked to put it, debriefing. Military Intelligence, CIA, FBI. They were all there asking questions almost around the clock. The loss of an agent like Roca was a big deal. The existence of some kind of cabal within the intel community an even bigger one. There was getting at the truth, then there was, more importantly, stopping any possibility of a leak about what had really happened.

"Why don't they just give us polygraphs?"

"I think it's over now," Brock said. "You're just coming down from the whole thing. You sleep at all last night?"

"No. Tossing and turning. I think I'm wired so tight I can't unwind. What about you?"

"I live that way. You get wound up and it can take a long time to get unwound again. And the minute you even think of getting really relaxed, they sense it like a shark smells blood. They come knocking and you're on your way again to some other choice piece of conflicted real estate."

"You chose this career," Anna reminded him.

"I wouldn't have it any other way," he replied.

He turned down a narrow path and parked. "Well, here is paradise. What do you think?"

A quiet brook emptied into a pool surrounded by rock and tall palms. The dying light of day lasered the forest around them with slanting shafts of light. It was beautiful.

"You have good taste. Are you going to try to seduce me out here?"

"I'm going to give it my best shot."

"I'm a little nervous," she said. "This scar fetish of yours."

"It's just a come-on."

She laughed.

"Quick, what's so bad about a fetish if it brings people together?"

She looked over at him. He stared at her a moment with seriously soulful eyes, but not without a little twinkle of boyish playfulness in them. "I'll answer that later."

He produced a blanket, bottle of wine and some cheese and crackers.

"You do this for all the girls?" Anna asked.

"Just the important ones."

"I'm glad I live up to your standards."

"Believe me, you're a big step up."

Anna helped him lay the blanket out on the flattest and softest piece of ground. She was falling for this guy. It was happening so fast it scared her. She'd even feared after the debriefing he'd be gone and that would be that. She'd be on her way back to the States and he'd slip back into his shadow world and their paths might never cross again.

Brock had changed her. For better or worse, he'd taken her into a world she knew nothing about and it had pushed her to be something she never thought she could be, or wanted to be. But it was done. Now wasn't the time to deal with that. Now was the time to deal with something else.

They ate cheese and crackers, drank a bottle of wine and talked lazily about whatever came to their minds. Where and how they grew up, their dreams and sorrows. He was very easy to talk to and it was one of those deliciously placid, deep evenings where the world seemed at peace. The wonderful illusion of tranquillity and goodness riding on a soft warm breeze. A moment beyond fires and gunfights.

Then, when the probing, kidding around and flirting came to that certain point, they both knew it was time to start comparing scars.

Anna didn't remember later who actually started it, but soon after, they ended up naked in the pool, naked on the blanket, and then running around in the woods laughing and playing escape and evasion.

Then they were back on the blanket under the stars the air warm and soft. Brock was a very good lover, totally into her body, learning it, mastering it. And it wasn't long before there were few barriers. She was permitting him anything he wanted. And there was almost no part of him left to her imagination.

Brock devoured her from head to toe, stopping, exploring, moving on. He wanted all of her and she let him have it. And when she was arching and moaning, coming to a rising crescendo, he'd change course, let her halfway down, then take her in a new direction to new heights, until they totally exhausted one another. All the days and nights of tension flowed out of their bodies and left them spent and satisfied.

Laying in his arms, remembering a picture, Anna chuckled out loud. Brock turned his head. "What?"

"Nothing."

"C'mon, what?"

"When you first walked in the water and stood there with nothing on but your ball cap. It reminded me of a picture that went around the Internet a bunch of years ago. This shot of a naked cowboy standing in a stream. He might have been fishing."

"He have great scars?"

"No. But like you, he had a sweet ass."

"Don't get started. Believe me, I've got nothing left."

Anna rolled over and put a leg up over his thigh. She rubbed the hair on his chest, then drew her finger down the scar on his lower abdomen.

She bit his earlobe, then nibbled his neck. "Bet I can make a liar out of you."

"I'm here. I'll take care of it."

Matt. His voice. Felt like a shower of gravel pelting my back. I turned around, winced. He was gowned, maskless, his handsome face sallow, pinched. It was his eyes that worried me. The sea-green, perpetually alert probes were turbid, spaced out.

Nope. He hadn't calmed down. Man. Like I needed this. My best friend and surgeon tripping on stress hormones.

But riding the adrenaline breakers while extracting our casualties from the midst of the white-slavery-auction-turned-turf-war hadn't been bad. I had to admit, his berserker violence had gotten us out in one piece. Yeah, then it had almost gotten us killed, when he'd taken the wheel of our escape van, putting a new spin-out-*and*-crash on the phrase "narrow escape." Still couldn't believe we weren't all lying there on the OR tables beside comatose, battered Juan and Mercedes.

I sighed as he passed behind me. Time to count our blessings and our in-one-piece bones and tell him to sit this one out. No way was he performing brain surgery in this shape.

"We're fine here," I said. "Juan's BP's going up, so's his cerebral perfusion pressure. We'll get him stabilized, then we'll review his CTs, decide how to proceed..."

Did he just ignore me? Yep. Still upset over my vocal criticism of his demolition-derby driving? Probably. Goodie.

He picked a pin, ran in on the insides of Juan's arms, conducting another neuro exam. Good idea—*if* he wasn't scraping his skin. Even from here, I saw scratches forming. On the last sweep across Juan's inner thigh, he drew blood. The hairs on my nape erupted on end. Matt didn't make mistakes like that!

It took the others swinging what-the-hell gazes from him to me to make me believe he just had. His pin was going deeper when I swooped down and snatched it away. "What are you *doing?*"

He just murmured, to himself it seemed, "Abnormal flexion and unilateral posturing. Must drill him open."

I snorted. "Yeah, sure. Why stabilize him and consult CTs when we can just drill him blind and finish him off right away? Okay, Matt, you've had it for tonight. Go sleep it off."

That was harsher than I intended. Guess I'd reached my limit for the night, too.

Matt did more than ignore me this time. His green gaze swung up, slammed into me. Everything inside me dimmed, cringed. Never thought I'd ever be on the receiving end of his wrath. I opened my lips, something confused and concerned forming there.

He just rammed it down my throat.

The shock hit first. And far harder. Then like a hurtling missile, the bone-cracking force of his double blows registered.

My brain scraped against my skull. Reality wavered. Jagged pain burst, more behind my ribs than in my shoulder and jaw. I clung to his arm, instinctive, my mind crashing, refusing to process the situation, his actions. *Please. Not Matt.*

He pushed me, his massive body seeming to expand, his fury liver colored, and appalling sound spilling from him. I staggered back and he charged after me, snatched me up by the arms and hurled me away. I sailed back, too enervated to twist into a safe landing. I slammed to the polished OR floor, right hipbone first, skidded, only the head-first collision into the autoclave aborting my momentum.

My consciousness flickered on images of Fadel and Sam jumping Matt. A delirious wheeze wouldn't make it past my lips. *Not that way, you fools! He'll pulverize you.*

He did. The sickening sound of colliding flesh and bone reverberated in mine. Fadel launched back with the force of a blow that killed men, already unconscious. Sam was flung into the horrified team deep in Mercedes's cardiothoracic surgery. The chain reaction took down the anesthesia station—and Mercedes.

Time stuttered as she slumped off the table, slammed to the floor, disconnected from the heart-lung and anesthesia machines, her chest gaping wide, her heart exposed, her blood everywhere.

Okay, Calista St. James. You've cracked up.

Yeah, this was it. I had to be living my ultimate phobia. Another of my loved ones turning into a madman I had to stop. At any cost. *Somebody else do it this time—please!*

Nobody else. The others were struggling to restore Mercedes to the table, to straighten the upturned machines and replace the destroyed ones. Leaving Matt to me.

Matt and the burr-hole perforator he'd reached for.

It was plugged. He turned it on.

Go to pieces later. Stop him—now!

A scenario played in my mind. Skirting him, knocking the perforator away and… No. In his condition, engaging him would only earn us more injuries—or worse. No way could I subdue him without inflicting serious damage on him. Without maximum force…

No way. Never. Had to find another way. Had to.

I rose to my feet, injecting my movements with ease, forced to raise my voice over the perforator's marrow-drilling whine. "C'mon, Matt, don't be so angry with me. I'm sorry I snapped."

"I'm in charge," he rasped. Was that directed to me?

Didn't think so. I ventured another step toward him as he stared at the perforator wobbling furiously in his hand. "Sure, Matt. I was waiting for you to decide to take over."

He looked up, looking through me, his voice softening on a deluge of passion. "I'll never let you out of my sight. No one will ever touch you." He suddenly roared a hair-raising laugh. "I ripped you apart alive, made you watch and wait your turns. I do it again, every day. I dance over your severed parts."

God. This was definitely not directed at me. He was hallucinating. About his wife? And the vermin who'd kidnapped and raped her death? He'd caught up with them, gotten even. I hadn't asked how. So that was how. Was it why he'd snapped now?

No. I'd been there for him all through. He'd never lost coherence. Never turned on his friends. On me. Going psychotic wasn't in his makeup. This wasn't a breakdown. His pupils were dilated, he was sweating rivers. He was under the influence. Of what, I had to restrain him to find out, to counteract it. And he hadn't done this to himself. No freaking way. He'd been poisoned. How, who and what, I'd find out later.

Now maybe I could still reach him. "Let me help, please."

He shook his head, his voice a pitch-black, bleeding whisper. "None of it matters. I can't kill enough of them to bring her back, to say I'm sorry. *To make her screams stop.*"

Oh, *Matt...*

He raised the perforator. "But I've found the way. I have to drill it out of my brain. The pain, the rage."

He turned to Juan's limp, tube-infested body. "See how sick I look? Once it's drilled out of my brain, I'll be whole again." He nodded to himself, approached Juan in slow, determined steps.

A collective cry echoed. Lucia screamed. This was her brother lying there. I raised my hand. *Don't antagonize him.*

I took three more careful steps closer. "Let me help you, Matt. Give me the burr and I'll remove all your pain and rage."

He kept on going. Lucia whimpered, begged. I could no longer ask her silence. I shouted, a desperate last resort. "*Matt!* Turn that burr off. And step away from Juan. *Now,* Matt!"

He touched the perforator to Juan's head. We all exploded.

I reached him first, got folded over his foot, almost broke in two, slammed to the floor again. Lucia threw herself at the electric cord, got a vicious kick in the head, crumpled, blood seeping from her mouth. Sam fell screaming, the drill in Matt's hand splattering the tissue it had gouged out of his shoulder.

Something corrosive scorched down my middle, my cheeks.

"Take him down." I felt Ayesha press a dart gun in my hand.

I had them loaded with enough tranquilizer to fell two men. But there was no telling what Matt was high on. It was why I'd struck drugs off my list of options to subdue him. One more drug and I could cause him irreversible damage. Or kill him.

I raised the dart gun, pointed it straight at his jugular.

USA TODAY
BESTSELLING AUTHOR

Shirl HENKE

BRINGS YOU

SNEAK AND RESCUE
March 2006

Rescuing a brainwashed rich kid
from the Space Quest TV show
convention should have been a cinch
for retrieval specialist Sam Ballanger.
But when gun-toting thugs gave chase,
Sam found herself on the run with a truly
motley crew, including the spaced-out
teen, her flustered husband and one
very suspicious Elvis impersonator....

eHARLEQUIN.com

The Ultimate Destination for Women's Fiction

Your favorite authors are just a click away
at www.eHarlequin.com!

- Take a sneak peek at the covers and
  read summaries of **Upcoming Books**

- Choose from over 600
  author **profiles!**

- Chat with your favorite authors
  on our **message boards.**

- Are you an author in the making?
  Get advice from published authors
  in **The Inside Scoop!**

**Learn about your favorite authors
in a fun, interactive setting—
visit www.eHarlequin.com today!**

Silhouette® BOMBSHELL™

BOUNTY HUNTER.
HEIRESS.
CHANTAL WORTHINGTON WAS

HELL ON HEELS

by Carla CASSIDY

Chantal was on familiar terrain
when she went after a fellow blue blood
who'd skipped bail on a rape charge.
But teaming up with bounty hunter
Luke Coleman to give chase was a
new move in her playbook. Soon things
were heating up on—and off—the case....

Available March 2006